PENGUIN BOOKS

An Innocent Gentleman

Elizabeth Jolley was born in the industrial Midlands of England and moved to Western Australia in 1959. She is acclaimed as one of Australia's leading writers and has received an Order of Australia, and honorary doctorates from WAIT (now Curtin University), Macquarie and Queensland universities and the University of New South Wales. She has also received an honorary professorship from Curtin University and the ASAL Gold Medal for her contribution to Australian literature, as well as many major Australian awards for her fiction.

Elizabeth Jolley's work includes short fiction, a collection of essays and fifteen novels, of which *The Well* won the Miles Franklin Award, *Mr Scobie's Riddle* and *My Father's Moon* the *Age* Book of the Year Award and *The Georges' Wife* the National Book Council award for fiction.

ELIZABETH JOLLEY

Hazel and
signed for B & B copy

An
Innocent
Gentleman

13 April 03

PENGUIN BOOKS

Penguin Notes for Reading Groups are available at www.penguin.com.au

Penguin Books

Published by the Penguin Group
Penguin Books Australia Ltd
250 Camberwell Road
Camberwell, Victoria 3124, Australia
Penguin Books Ltd
80 Strand, London WC2R 0RL, England
Penguin Putnam Inc.
375 Hudson Street, New York, New York 10014, USA
Penguin Books Canada Limited
10 Alcorn Avenue, Toronto, Ontario, Canada M4V 3B2
Penguin Books (N.Z.) Ltd
Cnr Rosedale and Airborne Roads, Albany, Auckland, New Zealand
Penguin Books (South Africa) (Pty) Ltd
24 Sturdee Avenue, Rosebank, Johannesburg 2196, South Africa
Penguin Books India (P) Ltd
11, Community Centre, Panchsheel Park, New Delhi 110 017, India

First published by Penguin Books Australia 2001
This paperback edition published 2002

1 3 5 7 9 10 8 6 4 2

Cover design by Lynn Twelftree and Sandy Cull, Penguin Design Studio
Cover illustration by Priscilla Nielsen
Text design by Sandy Cull, Penguin Design Studio
Typeset in Goudy by Post Pre-press Group, Brisbane, Queensland
Printed and bound in Australia by McPherson's Printing Group, Maryborough, Victoria

National Library of Australia
Cataloguing-in-Publication data:

Jolley, Elizabeth, 1923- .
An innocent gentleman.

ISBN 0 14 300066 7.

I. Title.

A823.4

www.penguin.com.au

ACKNOWLEDGEMENTS

I would like to express my thanks to Curtin University of Technology for the continuing privilege of being with students and colleagues in the School of Communication and Cultural Studies, and for the provision of a room in which to write.

A special thanks is offered to Kay Ronai for editorial advice and corrections. Special thanks as well to Nancy McKenzie who continues to type my manuscripts.

And to all at Penguin Books Australia: thank you.

Dramatis Personae

All characters represented in this novel have a variety of reasons for being, some relationships being well known and others somewhat hidden. They are:

Mr and Mrs Henry Bell

Their two little girls

Victor

Mr H. or Mr Hawthorne – more later.

Mme D. Tonkinson (Private Home Masseuse, Dressmaking and Hairdressing, Ladies Only)

Miss Dotty Whatsaname T., daughter of the above. Personal ambition: to be a film star.

SETTING: The industrial Midlands, England.

TIME: Some time in the middle of the domestic side of life during World War Two.

'I'll get him! I'll get that man. That Mr Hilter, who does he think he is in any case?'

'Er, the name is Hitler and he's all bunkered up, you'll never get him.'

Scottish voice off – 'Shut up the both of you, it's this book I want to read, not *about* the war but only in the war because there's a war on . . .'

The mind of man is fram'd even like the breath
And harmony of music. There is a dark
Invisible workmanship that reconciles
Discordant elements, and makes them move
In one society.

The Prelude
W. WORDSWORTH

$\mathcal{H}$enry allowed his wife seven items on her dressing table, items which could be moved easily and returned as necessary when Henry cleaned and used the dressing table. He had it in mind to write a novel of thought and feeling and the suggestions put forward by Dostoevski in his letter to a young mother shortly before he died.

During a war, Henry continued his enlightening remarks from one day to the next. During a war, a man, leaving his family, with no alternative choice, might be recruited and put in a uniform and sent to some isolated coast somewhere in Britain or in Europe. And when, ultimately, face to face with his superior officer, the officer in charge would expect the new recruit to recognise his own formal greeting of the salute. The new recruit would be expected to be in uniform. Refusal to put on the uniform would be described as insubordination and this carried a gaol sentence.

Wherever the recruit would be sent, the salute was the gesture of respect and faith, the prescribed movement in which the whole body was involved . . . A prescribed movement belonging to a certain discipline, demonstrating a belief, and a complete faith in the wholesomeness of the continuing operations. From the most Senior and Experienced to the youngest, lately arrived recruit . . .

Often, the outward and visible material signs and symbols of happiness and success only show themselves when the process of decline has already set in . . .

Buddenbrooks

THOMAS MANN

He said the subtlest thing of all: that the lover was nearer the divine than the beloved; for the God was in the one but not in the other – perhaps the tenderest, most mocking thought that ever was thought, and source of all the guile and secret bliss the lover knows.

Thought that can emerge completely into feeling, feeling that can emerge completely into thought – these are the artist's highest joy.

Death in Venice

THOMAS MANN

Seating himself at the piano, he rubbed his hands together and held them massaged and poised above the keyboard. Henry, noticing the clean rosy fingers, saw as well the silent communication, the little glance which was a part of the tiny pause before the first notes, in a performance, were heard. The small but exclusively penetrating glance, he would tell Muriel later, between the visitor and Muriel, herself, followed by the tense almost sharp and authoritative nod, coinciding each in the other's direction, seemed like a secret language, enfolded in the body, without which the music could not be played.

But there was more than this. He discovered within seconds, there was something more.

$\mathcal{H}$enry noticed that after the playing of the Beethoven sonata, a part of this delicate sonata, in the moment of silence following the music, Mr Hawthorne, turning from the piano, had in a rather intimate movement lifted with one finger a strand of Muriel's hair, gently placing it behind her left ear. It seemed to Henry then that he was noticing for the first time that his wife's ears were very small and very pretty. And the movement of Mr Hawthorne's finger, while being restrained and gentle, combining his well-bred elegance and his tenderness, was possibly a part of a secret possessiveness as he then withdrew his finger, at the same time gently stroking the smooth roundness of her cheek with his fingertips. A silent moment of farewell as if keeping her beside him, sweetly close after their music-making . . .

Henry saw this modest little scene as a part of the

music and now as an expression of the desire for perfection in their performance, and their pleasure, their *obvious* pleasure, at the harmony produced between them in such an apparently simple way. Henry was deeply touched by the power in the ending of the sonata, the consonance, the deeply felt agreement. With his own complete possession of Muriel he could afford to be generous with an expression of freedom for both musicians, temporarily, as he explained (wordlessly) to himself, while the effects of the music were still present.

Mr H., Mr Hawthorne, must visit often. He decided he would say this later. First, he would think about it.

$\mathcal{H}$e seemed to be always on the pavement ahead of her, as if by chance, or at the bus stop. Because of the war he did not have a car (no petrol), but a car was available for him when required. He never said anything about this, but, when necessary, simply explained in a matter-of-fact sort of way. He seemed, he said, to be always walking. He rather enjoyed walking. Giving up the car was no hardship.

Following Mr Hawthorne, she thought about his unexpected visit the previous afternoon. He had come there to their house, by accident, he explained to Henry, who was at the time trimming the stunted hedge which grew along the low brick wall at the front of the house. 'Out of curiosity,' he said, causing Henry, as he told Muriel later, some surprise.

I mean, Henry had said, it was surprising that anyone, especially someone like him, would come to look at a newly built, low-rental housing estate in the hopes of discovering, and this was Henry's own thought, in the hopes of discovering a little nucleus of culture; perhaps some music or, in another language, some poetry or a part of a romantic novel, unfinished, and in such an unlikely place. After all this man did not need to *search*, he lived in the warm comfort within the elevated culture, within reach of his own chosen friends. And he was once more taking the advantage of evening classes, as if he needed them!

He, Mr Hawthorne, said that he had never really visited this place, during the day, except to their house, on the edge of the estate, when they had so kindly invited him to a Christmas drink along with other students from Mrs Bell's evening language class. He had only really seen the place late at night when seeing someone safely home in his capacity of voluntary ARP Warden, he added with a restrained little laugh, that sort of thing. And that was only once or twice a week when he took his turn with other wardens. As he spoke he glanced at Muriel and smiled.

Henry, he told Muriel later, Henry found himself on that day, fondly watching this man as he entered the house at his, Henry's, invitation. Really fondly, Henry insisted, like, he said, like love at first sight, which was a terrible cliché, when you thought about it. But there he was handsome and noble, large in their small sitting room where the little girls and their mother were practising, with violins and the piano, a Beethoven sonata.

Well, it wasn't *first sight* exactly, Henry *gave in* later, when confronted. But a sort of first sight of *innocence*.

The recently invited guest, almost at once, asked if he could have the honour of accompanying a violinist. He wasn't, he said in his pleasant voice, anything out of the ordinary on the piano. He had been told, at one time, that he had supple fingers which were useful. And, he added, he had played hymns for his aunts. They, of course, were completely uncritical. He hoped that his request was not impertinent.

'Henry,' Muriel's quiet voice roused Henry from a sudden forgetfulness, 'you remember,' she went on, 'this is Mr Hawthorne from the evening class. *Remember?*'

Mr Hawthorne, seating himself at the piano, rubbed his hands together and held them massaged and poised above the keyboard. Henry, noticing the clean rosy fingers, saw as well the silent communication, the little glance which was a part of the tiny pause before the first notes in a performance were heard. The small but exclusively penetrating glance, he would tell Muriel later, between the visitor and Muriel herself, followed by the tense almost sharp and authoritative nod, coinciding each in the other's direction, seemed like a secret language, enfolded in the body, without which the music could not be played.

The two little girls, nursing their violins, gazed at the floorboards and at their sandals, which were suddenly, it seemed, familiar and lovable in their well-worn shabbiness. They, the little girls, Henry noticed, seemed to have an understanding of the moment (something else to tell Muriel), and an understanding of the way in which the music filled the whole room in an anticipation of perfection. A transformation, a rare thing in such a nondescript room. He thought he would mention that as well.

Husband and wife, knowing each other with complete intimacy, could later agree about the responsibility
of the lover, the well-educated, well-bred lover who pos-
sesses the secret joy of being nearest and the most
powerful participant in this brief and tender meeting.

Husband and wife could, because of previous times,
tell each other how the feelings of love can merge simultaneously with the most private thoughts of love. The
ardent and sometimes elusive consummation, when it
comes, being for them at the time the most important,
the most precious moments of all time. Each receiving
the homage paid by the other.

Husband and wife would see, both of them, the competent hands, the fingers poised and flexible; and both
husband and wife would know that in certain music and
certain performance it was possible to feel these hands
as if they were caressing shoulders, breasts and thighs,
wandering gently as a part of the desired homage . . .
the reverence. Even more closely Henry and Muriel
would know because they had talked together in the dark
about this.

Then again, there was the thought that Henry had invited the guest, Mr Hawthorne, in at sunset, during the prettiest glow of sunset, interrupting the children at their music practice, and then inviting him to supper.

'You'll stay for some supper?' Henry caught the anxiety in Muriel's eyes. He had forgotten that there was very little food in the house.

Muriel understood at once that the guest was unable to stay. He was too polite and far too well bred to inconvenience them. She, the wife, watched her husband guiding the guest from the small room into the quickly darkening and mean little hall. She had to understand, and did understand, something she could see of a possessive tenderness, a kind of pleasure in being attentive to the visitor. Henry, it seemed, was almost patting Mr Hawthorne to the front door. From his actions and the tone of his voice it was clear, as she would say later, that Henry inwardly admired this man and did not attempt to hide this admiration. Perhaps it was more than just admiration, perhaps it was a possessive tenderness. He was allowing himself, in the modern way, to be free with feeling and demonstration of affection (it was the war, men kissed each other in the street, when meeting or saying goodbye). Another subject for the little talks in the dark, whispers really, the little girls sleeping so near.

Perhaps she was mistaken, but it seemed that Henry, in his attention to Mr Hawthorne, for example, his bending down and lightly brushing with one hand the tired flower petals from his visitor's trousers (the path being so narrow), that Henry might have a generous feeling towards small boys at some time in his teaching experience. These would be small boys from the same stock that produces the Mr Hawthornes. These would be boys quite different in their attributes, different in physical grace and strength and sensitive academic possibilities from the boys with whom he spent his life, his interests and his energy – at present.

She nodded to herself, seeing a better school, a vivid picture in her mind. She sent the little girls upstairs to wash themselves and sat listening as the two men lingered, she presumed, at the gate, as they wished each other a good night. Henry, she thought, might have

measured himself, perhaps finding himself 'wanting'.
Perhaps he secretly dreamed of teaching in a completely
different environment; a school in which he would be
expected (to his delight) to teach contemporary literature with a well-made background – Chaucer and
Shakespeare and many of the famous novelists and
poets. It would be a school where the school orchestra
played Mozart and Beethoven *and* Vaughan Williams. A
school where well-mannered boys shook hands after a
fight; the boys themselves would be single-minded in
their ambitious thoughts towards being Officers and
Gentlemen.

It was possible, Muriel thought, that Henry might wish
to teach and have a fatherly interest in boys from the kind
of background enjoyed by Mr Hawthorne when he was a
boy. *A man must father that which he has been able to produce.*
Muriel was not sure what she meant with the words. They
sounded, when she said them aloud, like an important rule
for living. Her mother could well have made a statement
of that sort, with bits of it in French and German.

'What did you come back inside for?' she called out

to Henry after the gate had clicked shut behind Mr Hawthorne.

'I'm lending him George Orwell,' Henry replied.

'Which one?'

'*Burmese Days* and the others, the lot.'

Henry went upstairs to wash and to send the children down to their bread and jam and cocoa.

'Who was that man?' the elder little girl asked while they were having supper.

'I like him for mine,' the younger one said.

'He's not *that man*,' Henry saw the need for correction, 'he is a gentleman. And don't speak, either of you, with your mouths full.'

Later Henry told Muriel that she and Mr Hawthorne played the sonata together very well. 'It was beautiful,' he said, his voice deep with an inexplicable rush of emotion.

'It was only a part of it,' she said.

'It was enough,' he said.

Henry was never all that keen on music, Muriel thought, there was always something more to find out about him. All the same she could not resist saying that Mr Hawthorne probably had all Orwell's books as well as a great many by other authors. Later she wished she had not made the unnecessary remark.

It was the new neighbour, Mrs Tonks, and her daughter Miss Tonks, who, coming home from the city market one Saturday, brought a shoe box containing two baby guinea pigs. One each, Mrs Tonks told them, one each for each of the two little girls. The neighbour explained that the little creatures were orphans and they would need mothering. They would need a hutch of some kind but perhaps the father was good with his hands?

One of the awkward things about moving into the new house, Henry and Muriel, after having no neighbours, discovered that they now had neighbours, though most of the new houses were not yet ready for inhabitants. Henry was mainly pleased that the house was somewhat isolated. He was, as well, delighted in the fact that it was a new, previously unlived-in house, everything being new and clean.

'There are no shelves and no cupboards,' Muriel said. Henry said he would remind the rent collector when he called on Monday evening. Meanwhile they would keep their things in boxes.

The neighbours, as it turned out, occupied a house on the same bulge and curve of the new housing estate. They were easily within walking and calling distance. Calling as applied to the voice, to shouting encouraging greetings rather than actually dropping in. The habit of dropping in wasted time, Henry said, it was best not to encourage it.

Just give a shout, he told Muriel, when you are near the gate or the dustbins. Be friendly but cautious.

The road to the other houses was unfinished as were many of the roads across the entire estate. Unfinished roads of clinker and tar macadam, Henry explained in a little breakfast-time lecture, were very rough to fall on. The children must take care not to run and fall. Macadam, he told them, was a thick, black, messy stuff used for preserving road materials and the timber used in ship building. He told them that, because of the war, he doubted that the road building would be finished for the time being. Henry had recently been given permission to teach his little daughters at home, there not being a school near by. It must, he said, be remembered yet again that the country was at war with Germany. The declaration of war, he said, was an intrusion, an excuse and a promise which was broken. And promises, he added, were made often and not kept.

The war would probably hold up the building of some of the houses. Henry said that he felt they were among the fortunate ones, being almost the first to move in.

The new estate was separated from an ancient leafy, mellow suburb by a little-used ring road.

The little creatures, the little pets, seemed to enjoy being dressed up in dolls' clothes, some of which were real babies' clothes carefully hoarded by Muriel while under the serious, in her case, belief that the minute you gave away the pram and the cradle and a pile of 'hardly worn' baby clothes, you at once fell pregnant (her own phrase) and were quite unprepared for the event of yet another baby.

Hang on to all those things, let them fill the house and you would never need them again . . .

The little creatures, the little furry pigs, were dressed each in a lacy baby gown, and, as well, a tiny bonnet, all of which were too big, and the animals, slipping down inside their clothes, were just able to peer out upon the world with a gaze both mischievous and perplexed.

The girls took turns to push the dolls' pram. They crossed the stream by the footbridge and walked on by the water where it flowed between the grassy banks in the first of the three fields.

All at once, as if the guinea pigs were able to know and recognise the delights of running water, they wriggled and twisted in their Christening gowns. And, then with a series of troubled attempts, they managed to escape from the pram. They were over the side and hurtling down the steep bank. The children watched the gowns and bonnets floating and then sinking as if the water would soon be swallowing their defenceless pets.

'Them babbies them'll be drownded dead in a minute or two.' A big boy, crouching, was suddenly close beside them. 'Aw, don't you cry,' he said, 'hold yer noise while I grab 'em.' His name was Victor, he said, he told them to keep quiet. He scrambled down the bank and grabbed quickly at the sinking clothes. In no time at all he had undressed the animals. He handed the girls the soaked gowns. 'Best let them little watter rats go free,' he said.

The girls, pulling the pram together, hurried home. Henry said that a more natural life was better for the animals. Muriel said they were rodents and, as such, did not mix well with human beings.

$\mathcal{T}$he schoolmaster, Henry, while sitting later than he intended to sit, on a Sunday morning, at his wife's dressing table in the shared bedroom, remembered reading somewhere that Samuel Johnson had been afraid to write his *History of Melancholy* because it would 'too much disturb him'. And in subsequent reading Mr H. Bell, Henry (schoolmaster), found the same sentiments expressed by Sir Walter Scott in his journal, 23rd May 1830 (discontinued for nearly a year): 'I thought it made me abominably selfish, and that by recording my gloomy fits I encouraged their recurrence.' He put aside the books and took up his pen to write that he was glad to know of the sorrows of these two worthy men and that, since reading these passages, he was not alone now with his own grievances.

The bedroom was superficially tidy; shoes, clothes and other things having been pushed into the cheap wardrobe, and the fitted bed quilt was stretched tight across the lumpy unmade bed.

Sitting later and later, useless and disappointed with himself, not able to create a poem when he had so many ideas and a selection of rhyming words and phrases at his disposal, Henry had to agree with himself that disappointment with the self is the worst kind and entirely unproductive. Setting oneself to achieve more than is possible and then falling short repeatedly has a very bad effect. He really needed a healing poem.

Determined to actually use the time for something he took the two notebooks, which he kept neatly on a little shelf at the side of the dressing table. In the first notebook he recorded the date and the pound note which would be the housekeeping money for the forthcoming week. He put the money in a jar reserved for housekeeping expenses. He then opened the notebook kept for Muriel's secret inner life and recorded her latest period and the number of days. This being a service which, he often said, should be provided by all men for their women, this last being a sort of 'use of language joke'; use of language, punctuation, tense and the plural.

Muriel was hopeless about her own body and its functions. 'Periods,' Henry thought and felt, were over-generous and used as a weapon at times. He resolved, in silence, to teach his daughters, when the time came, how to deal with and look after their own sweet little bodies.

Because Muriel was never prepared for her 'time of the month' (her use of the well-known phrase), Henry kept notes. She was often angry at these times. Henry did the special shopping for these occasions and came home with a soft brown-paper parcel under one arm, his attaché case being too full of schoolbooks and papers. He kept the records neatly in his careful handwriting. A handwriting similar to that of doctors and lawyers.

'One should keep away from a man with this hand-writing.' Muriel's mother had no reservations or difficulties about saying exactly how she felt about any person or other subjects, the war, conscription, refugees, rationing and her son-in-law. Endlessly she dragged out the subject of the war, taking up certain issues, dropping them, taking them up again as a dog drops his bone in order to pick it up just once more.

The war was well under way with air-raid warnings, the sirens being followed in due course by the long drawn-out 'All Clear'.

Muriel said, because Henry had already said it before, that people should, because of the dreadful uncertainty about life and sudden death, people should do as they pleased because on the next day they might be killed.

'So,' Muriel's mother said, 'they will marry the wrong man because of an air-raid warning?' She shrugged her thin shoulders and made her mouth into a thin line.

Henry, the peacemaker, taking every opinion Muriel's mother put forward as seriously as possible, joined her in listing the smaller, but by no means in her opinion, useless products necessary for a war. 'There are,' he agreed, 'the gas masks, the grey blankets, the ration books, the aluminium plates and mugs, the blackout material and the cancelled – at the last minute – transport, and, at the last minute, Identity Cards . . .'

'British Restaurants,' his mother-in-law shuddered and then added to her list, 'boarded-up premises and, on all sides, uniforms and accents.'

'Accents,' Henry jumped in on them, emerging as men and women in uniform being moved from one end of Great Britain to the other . . .

'And back,' his mother-in-law could never hold her tongue, always spending time and energy on telling people to hold theirs. The accessories of the war became between them a chanting, a crooning, a lullaby. Muriel's mother and Muriel both had singing voices innocently weak enough for singing games and nursery rhymes. Together they sang the next list; the Land Army, the ATS (Auxiliary Territorial Service). Henry's voice, providing a descant, enhanced the rather dreary and dreaded ARP (Air Raid Precautions) and the NA (the Nursing Auxiliary).

'That's mine,' Henry would strike his breast. 'My Solo, the Naughty Annies, the nurses . . .'

'Time for your baths.' Calling up the stairs to the children, Henry would, as usual, tell them it was the end of Sunday and that he was going to the bus stop, his wife on one arm and his mother-in-law on the other. 'Back soon, be very quick to bed!, or else I beat your mother!'

Henry understood that for Muriel's mother the 'better class' service was the Women's Royal Naval Service. Better class socially, enjoying the Club life and knowing people with titles and praising wines they knew to be good and so favoured. Club laughter was hard and brittle, Henry would never be able to share a joke with anyone in the Club. Fortunately he knew this. He never discussed the Club life with anyone but was able to identify, at a glance, one of Them or a bunch of Them. He shaped Them for himself to see Them as They were. He knew in advance that, on retirement from the particular position in the Services, they would choose to live in a Retirement Village (near golf and riding), and enjoy everyday meetings, at about half-past five, in the Club where they would drink (modestly), have some conversation and laughter, a meal and dancing. The retirement village essentially would supply everything as a war does for social mingling with the right people. Club life accepted that wars, a world of war, consisted essentially of a few polished tables in London, in Berlin and Paris, where men sat and made decisions, in particular which other men were ready to be 'sent to the front'.

Many people, Henry thought, had not known what friendship and good times were till they were a part of the war – meeting in the Club. This was their way of seeing and having a war. To him it was harmful, even destructive, in spite of the right accent and the superior education and family background.

Henry, foolishly, tried to push his point of view without seeing he was talking to two bored women.

Somewhat overcome with some sort of curious emotion, Henry said he was sorry. And leaving the two women to quarrel over the bus timetable, he went home and up to the dressing table as quickly as he could.

Fortunately the two little girls were together in the other bed, in the other room, asleep.

Unable to sleep (he should not have deserted Muriel), he thought about the rash of posters and notices intended to encourage and educate, to enliven and exhilarate the entire population with heart-warming slogans and educational messages, especially those giving the positive impression that the British would win the war. (*Muriel might be walking home from the bus stop, might be an air-raid. He should not have left the two women . . .*) Most people, Henry told himself, did not read or think much but quoted the latest poster, advertisement or headline. He wondered why he tried to write poetry. He thought about the healing quality he tried to bring to the pages. Whoever would read him? He would enlarge on these thoughts in the other notebook.

He thought about Muriel. Why did they invite her mother on their one, so-called, free day? He could not help thinking about Muriel. He wanted to know, every minute, what she was thinking about. He noticed that she looked as if she had been crying, or as if she wanted to cry. He did not feel strong enough for grief, real or imagined. He was sure he was not guilty of causing her grief. He reached for the shelf on the dressing table. He consulted her dates. Period finished two days ago, this would be one of her better nights, when desire was intense . . .

Henry dressed himself quickly (he must find Muriel), she should be home by now. He hurried, his mind filling with poetic phrases, he needed an – or rather one – ominous sound, an idea, a magic phrase for expression, that was all. Being at war with Germany meant a certain responsibility of thought about the two countries, and about the young men, the embodiment of this war, called up from the cities, the towns and villages, and perhaps never to return. The poetry required something else; the magic and the excitement of the spice-warm fresh bread, the fragrance of coffee and cigars in the streets where the chairs and tables were on the pavements. The sound of German voices, he could recall it all, German sausage and sauerkraut, the perfume from that other country.

Henry caught Muriel at the end of the street where the new estate met the main road. He caught her in his arms and they ran together as in a three-legged race (the pet race for all teachers in poor districts, no equipment is needed, the boys and the girls can use their own legs). Muriel and Henry matched well always in this race and this time was no exception. They ran without needing to tie their legs.

Repeatedly Henry remembers the smiling eagerness of a young saleswoman helping him to choose a tie to take back to his (then) headmaster. Since this was the first time, the first attempt, at taking a group of boys from the school to a chosen city in Europe, a gift seemed suitable.

'*Heil Hitler*,' the fresh-faced young girl said as she handed the neat little package to him, perhaps fore-telling misfortune. He supposes now that he should not have returned the greeting but at the time it seemed natural, a gesture of goodwill, before any war, on both sides.

'*Echte Seide*,' the girl smiled and nodded at the pack-age. In any case he was spending his own money, not the school's money, on the headmaster – of all things!

Muriel has been sweetly asleep for some time curled within the curve of his own position. He wonders why, after their love-making he found it necessary to tell her about the pure silk tie which he purchased for the head-master and then was too shy to present it to him.

For some reason sleep has deserted him. He gives himself up to remembering his own elation, the passport and things like the 'customs' and the sounds of foreign languages. The warm 'foreign' air in the small market town is unforgettable for him, smelling as it did of farm animals, spilled beer and, above all, the lilacs which were all in flower. A profusion of white and blue leaning over fences so that the person on the footpath was forced into their exotic embrace.

Now, in contrast, the air would be heavy, sullen with fuel for the heavy tanks. All the time now the tanks would be rumbling through the innocent cobbled streets, one after the other on their way to the coast because the English are sure to invade sooner or later.

In years to come, Henry guessed, it would be the noise of these heavy vehicles, the tanks which people would talk about, and of course the various sounds of the enemy aircraft. Reminders of the war. Threatening.

It seemed to Henry, at odd times, for example, on his bicycle ride to school, that the war divided people by rank. He wanted to include something of this in his War Poems, and especially to make some notes for discussion with Muriel. He knew that during the Great War if a man refused to put on his uniform he could be put in prison for months, years even. His crime being disobedience and insubordination. He understood that this would not be the case at the present time. There were other aspects of change which, if suitably veiled, could be written in his poems. One change was that fighting from the sky had replaced the trenches of World War One. Men would not be sent, on foot, over the top. Their feet would not be sodden, unwashed and rotting in their boots. This seemed hardly the material for the poem he wanted to write. Fighting from the sky was more harmful and destructive to buildings, factories, crops and to people and their homes.

The war divided people by birth, education and rank. Every man. Every man of ordinary rank was obliged to salute those of a higher rank. He tried to think clearly but Muriel was in his mind. Muriel seemed, at present, to be preoccupied and sad. She was unapproachable, but, he reasoned in silent thought, he could wait. He had endless patience. Look at the mornings, the Sunday mornings, not a word on the pages. A notebook needs gentle ammunition . . .

This dividing of society by military rank was unsuitable. Every man of ordinary rank had to salute those of higher rank, who were, in their turn, setting up the simultaneous rigid greeting. Much time was used on both sides to fulfil the duty of the pause, the acknowledgement, the recognition and the salute whenever it came about, face to face or merely in passing, confrontation, or from across the street.

To think he was over there so immediately before the war with 'his boys'. So immediately and unthinkable. He wondered if any of them thought about this now.

$\mathcal{I}$t was nearly the end of the summer, an evening, light, still and warm, carrying the scents of flowers, dried, left over from the first richness of the season together with the sweetness of mown grass, slowly turning brown, in neat little suburban heaps and ridges. The hawthorn hedges were already bright with the shining red berries of autumn.

The two sisters agreed to go looking for birds' nests with the big boy who told them his name was Victor. He said to follow him down the road a bit to where it ended in the fields on the edge of the new housing estate.

There was a brook flowing in a big concrete pipe under the road, and then the water, slipping from the end of the pipe, made its way between grassy banks through the first of the three fields which had escaped from being taken over for new houses and rough, unfinished new roads.

'We're not allowed in the drain,' the elder sister explained since the big boy did not know them and so would not know what they were allowed and not allowed to do.

'We're not allowed in the drain,' she told him, 'we have to go over the little footbridge, we do.'

'That's orrite, youm not going in any watter,' Victor told them. 'Just going in them fields, we are, where there's hedges and bird nests.'

He told the sisters to stand, legs astride across the ditch where the brook water continued its journey. And, he said, they were to push with their hands and arms into the hedge, gently pushing the branches out of the way. He showed them how. He told them to whisper so as not to frighten the birds. 'And youm not to move sudden like and scary-cat the mother bird. Youse two youse look up in them branches.' He said 'branches' with the short 'a' which their mother always corrected, often regretting aloud her marriage to that common vowel, the short 'a'.

'Parth and barth, not path and bath,' she would say.

The same could be said, of course, about brarnches and branches.

'Youse two, yo look up in them branches,' Victor said, 'and I'll look down below.' He stepped right into the brook where the water came over the tops of his boots.

'Your feet will be dreadfully wet,' the elder sister said.

'That don't marrer,' Victor said. 'Yo want to see a bird nest dontcha? So don't talk out loud! Yo and your kiddie sister, yo look up above and I'll look down here under-neath.'

It was a funny thing, the sisters said, whispering, their voices cracking with the effort of whispering, this bird-nest hunt. Victor seemed all over the place, in the field, in the brook, in the hedge and in their clothes.

'He's under my frock,' one sister said to the other.

'And he's under mine and mine's all wet already,' the other replied. The sisters began to giggle helplessly.

'Funny Victor,' they said, and 'You are very very funny, Victor.'

'Hush yor noise, the both of you hush yor noise!' Victor was cross. In the ensuing silence the sisters heard their father whistling *Come to the cook-house door, boys* all across the stillness of the evening, *Come to the cook-house door, boys, come to the cook-house door.*

'That's our daddy.' The elder sister explained that their father whistled the tune without any words. 'He whistles for us to come home. He whistles from out our back bedroom window. I am so sorry we have to go now,' she said, smoothing her water-splashed dress. 'We have to go when he whistles,' she said, 'that house next to the end house is our house.'

'If I find a bird nest,' Victor promised, 'I'll keep a egg for youse tomorra or next week, I'll keep a bird egg each I will. The skylark,' he said. 'The skylark, her as sings up and up into heaven, her eggs is pretty and her nest, well, it's down in the grass of the field there, yo have to tek care not to step on the nest. I'll keep a egg each for you. I promise.'

'Thank you, Victor.' The sisters ran home quickly, calling 'Goodbye Victor' and not turning round once to see his bony, forever-starved arms and legs, and his eyes, slightly bulging, staring from his pale face.

The father (a thin man), while he ran the bath for the little girls, told them that they should be careful not to show their knickers and their thighs when they were playing in the fields. He made their warm milk and spread their pieces of bread and butter. He helped them to get dry, after their bath, by patting them ineffectually with their large but thin worn-out bath towels. Later he stood on the landing, at the top of the stairs, between the two bedrooms and read aloud in what the sisters called his school voice. He read the part in George Eliot's *Silas Marner* where Silas, by accident, breaks his earthenware jug while fetching water from the well. He realises he has lost 'a friend' and will never feel its handle on the palm of his hand again. But he takes up the pieces of the jug and props them up as a monument, though he knows he cannot fetch water in it again. The father saw this as an important note of optimism in the story and explained this to the little girls. Later on in his life everything will be happy and good for Silas.

Because of earaches, spiders, bad dreams and the various illnesses of childhood, the children slept in separate rooms, one with the father and the other with the mother. Affectionately the father has maintained the arrangement is an ideal form of contraception. He has said this in company judged carefully as suitable for such a remark. Nothing said in bad taste of course. Though it was known that there comes a time when certain things, if said too often between the same people, become merely repetitive, tiresome and meaningless.

Because of their qualifications, the father and mother are allowed to teach their two little girls at home. Later the father intends to send them to boarding school.

Their mother teaches evening classes. She teaches because the children's father, in his enthusiasm, signed up for evening classes but was unable to continue. He is teaching maths and science and supervising school dinners and sports every day, full time, at the Central School for Boys.

Because he was tired, the father only partly cleared up the kitchen. He never completed household tasks, this weakness made his wife, Muriel, wild. She could not stand coming home to the remnants of a meal and the unfinished washing-up, especially when he had been cooking kippers on a toasting fork over the open fire in the living room.

The father, dismissing his wife from his thoughts, took up his study book and began to read. After a bit his attention wandered from the text, *Geometry, Science of Properties and Relations of Magnitudes* . . . England was at war. He was lucky to be exempt to continue his teaching work *for the time being*. Apart from news about the actual fighting of the war, the effects of the war were showing already in what he considered to be the home details but important all the same. There were stories of refugees escaping and not knowing where their relatives were. Then there was the 'blackout' to be put up every evening and the worry about showing lights and the high-pitched neighbours like their Mrs Tonks and daughter Miss Tonks, who screamed that his lights showed all the way from the Midlands to the English Channel and beyond . . .

Suddenly everything was in short supply. There were well-mannered and patient queues everywhere for the bus, for greengroceries, for butcher's meat. It was also difficult to get a haircut and suddenly uniforms were very much in evidence. He thought about the uniforms, perhaps he should join the Auxiliary Fire Service or a First Aid Post. With Muriel being out at class some nights, they would have to ask Mrs Cox, the cleaning lady, to come in.

Damned nuisance this war, apart from the brutality, it was a nuisance ... He must have been sleeping in his chair and was awake now, disturbed; the children were not asleep in bed. He could hear them scampering across the linoleum. It was dark already and both children should have been asleep. He listened at the foot of the stairs. The children were excited. His wife would be tired and annoyed if they were still awake.

Upstairs, he found the children standing on the bed by the open window, they were leaning out of the window.

'Get back to bed at once,' he said.

'There's people on the bridge,' they told him.

'Back to bed, at once!' He snapped the words 'at once' at once, as if delivering a sharp slap, one each, to the children.

'There's lovers on the bridge, Daddy. Come and look.'

He told them again to get back to their own beds, or else!

He looked out of the window. He thought the woman was wearing a white hat.

'There's nothing there to worry about,' he said, his voice softening. The couple on the bridge, arms round each other, could not seem to part; though they seemed to have decided to each go their own way, they continued to hold hands. They were touchingly shy and romantic in the pale lamplight and the almost white light of a distant moon. The mist, rising from the grassy fields, gave the scene an ethereal delicacy to the impression, the idea, that the man and the woman were no longer young and that their embrace was a secret. The woman wore a long dark winter coat. He thought it might be buttoned up over a summer dress. Women wore coats wisely like this.

$\mathcal{I}$t was with difficulty that Muriel, the mother, found the second-hand bookshop. It was her idea to try to have a little extra money. It was reassuring to have enough and a little more than enough in her purse. The box of books was squeezed into a wire carrier on her bicycle. It was stupid, she knew, to pretend to herself that in selling the books (which all looked clean and fresh, some being new copies for 'review' – if Henry got around to it), she would soon save some money for a deposit on a car and, later, for a better house. Money was already owing on the piano and the three violins.

The shop was small and hidden between empty and partly demolished buildings. There was nowhere to put the bicycle and the box of books refused to be eased out of the carrier. She finally managed to prop the bicycle against the unwashed plate glass. A travel agent and estate agent had small offices, unattended, on either side of the bookshop. Two steps down from the footpath and then inside the shop she could not wait to climb out of it.

The rough narrow shelves and the frayed baskets of shabby books, the feeling of being shut in poverty, were all too much. She felt alone and helpless and depressed. She was unable to imagine the books finding a place in this shop and then, later, with someone who would cherish them.

She imagined her feelings to be those of a mother on leaving a graceful, well cared for and callow little child in the derelict yard of a school summer camp, especially if the little child was crying, begging not to be left, the little face flushed, full of grief and shame . . .

The owner of shabbiness was hidden behind a cloth screen. There was a sound as if someone was muttering over accounts. The mother, Muriel, did not wait to try in an unconvincing way to make a sale. She understood sadly that books, like unprofessional stamp collections, were impossible to sell. Books, people seemed to have the silent thought, books are for giving away. People expected to have books given to them. *I'll take them, these books, off your hands . . .*

The mother, longing to escape from the poor district, hoped that selling books and teaching evening classes would provide the money which could make changes in her life. She understood perfectly that these changes, so important to her, were not needed by her husband. His work in the Central School was a challenge for him, especially since his recent success with school dinners and dinner-time sports. He was a thin man with grey curls already showing in his unhealthy hair. The leather elbows in his second-hand jacket contributed to his appearance, 'pale and thoroughly washed out', as their neighbour, Mrs Tonkinson, described him to herself. Often, on occasions, forgetting that she was speaking to the man's wife, she would continue with her criticism: 'that man's eating his own heart out. He needs some good plain cooking and a proper turn-around holiday with a wife who's not afraid of the shared double bed.'

The father, the husband, thoroughly enjoyed teaching his own little girls. He made games with spelling and mental arithmetic and he read aloud from quite difficult books, whereas the mother felt only irritation with the children's appalling accents, which ruined the sound of simple sentences in French and German. The irritation caused her to say repeatedly that her back ached and that she was tired.

Then there was their piano practice, and then the visits to the Art Gallery and the Museum. The little girls had already started to run off and hide, to escape somewhere in the fields or along the unfinished roads, rough with clinker, and not leading anywhere. The children preferred the ugly housing estate and avoided the cultural extras which their mother hoped would lift them into a better class, a better way of living being able to be with better people.

'All this *better*,' the father said, prancing and then walking across the living room on his hands, 'stop thinking *better*.' He righted himself with a little jump. 'Stop this *better* thing and . . . Muriel, do stop and . . .'

'And what!' she screamed and was surprised at herself. 'And what! Mr Boring. Henry Boring Bradley Bell . . . What?'

'Well,' the father said, trying to explain, 'there is such a thing as enjoyment.'

The mother looked at the father. She saw him small and neat, methodical and hard-working. She knew how his grey eyes shone when he was preparing something for his boys at school, a visit to the town swimming baths, an educational journey down a coal mine or five days walking in the Austrian Tyrol. (Because of the war, Austria would have to give way to North Wales.) Her husband was a good and kind man. She knew this and burst into tears. He stood up and, closing the door, he took her in his arms, and, within his own restrictions, kissed her.

She, the mother, kept the distance as usual behind Mr Hawthorne, allowing herself the full pleasure of entering the classroom very quickly after his arrival.

Mr Hawthorne, she knew, would have played tennis in the afternoon and then, still at the Club, he would have had a bath and put on fresh clothes.

The mother, invited on one occasion, with the two little girls, watched him playing tennis. She saw, then, the grace and beauty and the correctness of his body, trained to be in perfect command of every kind of situation.

Briefly she allowed herself a few moments of imagining what it would be like to have Mr Hawthorne keeping his full weight from crushing her with his own passionate desire and, at the same time, caressing her own body, being sweetly serious and considering her before himself, and thinking what would be best and nicest for her. And sometimes, perhaps, he would be laughing, teasing her.

When he played tennis, it seemed that he played with the whole of his powerful, not so young, body. Powerful, agile and accurate. Restricted beads of moisture on his forehead being the only outward sign of the stress of the game, and at the same time demonstrating the superb control of his body, his thoughts and emotions.

It was impossible not to compare the years of good breeding in Mr Hawthorne's background with the meanly made body of her husband, who looked as if he had never, in his whole life (till the present), had enough to eat. But Henry, the husband, turned everything into a joke.

Later, on her way to the evening class, the mother saw the solid figure of Mr Hawthorne ahead of her. He must have been on the same bus. Mr Hawthorne was a Barrister by profession and a KC with chambers in the better part of the city. He was often a chairman of legal committees and he was on the Management Boards of a number of charities. He was a well-respected member of the Tennis Club and of the Bridge Club. And, among other things, he came from a long-established profes- sional family. He was a Church Warden and a bachelor and was looked after by an unmarried housekeeper, an elderly woman who had been with his mother's house- hold for as long as he could remember. And the husband, Henry, declared he was wasted. He would be a wonderful lover boy and he, Henry, felt quite at home, he said, if Muriel would be happier to have a lover boy. He, Henry, would turn a blind eye. Muriel told Henry to clear up the banal cliché-ridden words.

Mr Roderick Hawthorne was a valuable student in the mother's German Literature class, having come back a second year because of having enjoyed the first so much. His shy and graceful (for one who was stoutly built) speech and manner drew her to him at once, though he also confessed, on one occasion, in such an innocent *unmarried* way that *she caught him*, he found her irresistibly charming and that she made the German grammar into something memorable because it had *had to be learned*, compulsory and memorable and beautiful at the same time. He had to return, to re-enrol, because of this. And then there was the little sherry party before Christmas when the husband and father invited the handful of mature-age students to the house for a glass of Christmas sherry. During the evening Mr Hawthorne politely invited his host and his mentor to accompany him to the opera.

'Muriel would love that, thank you very very much,' her husband said and then explained that as Mrs Cox, their old Nanny, would be away he, Henry, would remain at home with the children.

The mother, grateful that her husband had been so agreeable, especially so since he elevated Mrs Cox from Cleaning Lady to Nanny, told Mr Hawthorne, later, that Henry did not really like or understand music and that, for her, going to a concert with someone for whom the music had no meaning and no real pleasure was a sheer waste. 'No magic,' she said then. Mr Hawthorne, holding her arm with affectionate fingertips, said that he agreed with her and he hoped, he said, that this visit to the opera would be the first of many.

Muriel and Henry decided that night at bedtime that as Mr Hawthorne seemed to be rather lonely they must be more friendly, and Henry suggested Sunday midday dinner after church and Muriel agreed. Not every weekend though, they agreed on that as well. Perhaps an open invitation once a month, Henry suggested, and we can discuss our relevant sermons with each other during the first course and, perhaps, predict the weather with the pudding.

'You can make a milk and water rice pudding in the bottom of the oven while the bit of meat and the potatoes are baking on the top shelf.' Henry was pleased with the idea. 'Tell you what,' he went on, 'himself, the Lover Boy, can practise his *Deutsch mit uns*, in private, because of the war. And I'll tell you more, we'll invite Mrs Tonks and the Tonkette from the house across the way!' Playfully he squeezed her breasts and waited for a kiss or a slap before leaving the other bedroom.

'And don't come back!' she hissed. 'And don't wake the children, singing in the bath the way you always do!'

$\mathcal{S}$unday red notebook: Muriel regular and not pregnant. Really our lives deal with the incommensurable but I would rather live than not. There is no other way of describing this. I am grateful for my marriage and more so having left the school in North London to come here to the industrial midlands. I feel I must warn Muriel. 'Muriel,' I shall say, 'be honest and understand that you are not Bridge material . . . and your clothes, all our clothes need replacing, even the teddy bears are bald and undressed. Stick with the tender music (Mozart) or the representative (Beethoven opera), the characters being as the composer thought they should be. *Keep the real wishes in the human heart. Remember this!'*

Prackerly on speaking terms with the Lady Tonks and her daughter Tonkette. Didn't realise Muriel's mother here already. She comes earlier and earlier! END H. Bell.

$\mathcal{H}$e seemed to be always ahead of her, on the pavement, as if by chance. Or he might be at the bus stop or at the railway station. Today he would be in the brass-bound shining doorway of the Lion Hotel restaurant, as if by chance, saying how glad he was that she had come because he needed his lunch. He wanted to know was HE (her husband) expected?

Laughing she would explain that HE was supervising the school dinners, regretting that he was not free to come. And then, in the same apparently unconcerned way, without any embarrassment, he would guide her exquisitely, as if with fingertips, to the table reserved for them.

During the meal he would, with some hesitation, speak German in his well-bred, well-modulated voice which was so perfectly English that she could not hide her admiration and pleasure, almost telling him outright that she loved him, he was so elegant and refined. His clothes, his clean, ironed shirts, and his ties, chosen with good taste, all with special tie-pins or buttons indicating allegiance to various orders and societies and honours; all these things added to the pleasure she had in his company. She told him and he listened, his good-natured face flushed and smiling opposite her.

The mother, the wife, Muriel wore her green winter coat, dark green and long, buttoned over summer dresses long since discarded in her mind, and dragged out with reluctance. She often, without realising it, buttoned and unbuttoned the coat, her fingers working nervously. With the green coat, which was not new, she wore a round white hat made of soft felt. A sort of Tammy, a Tam-o'-Shanter, no longer, if ever, fashionable, but originally of good quality.

On this day when they were having lunch (the little girls were at home with chicken pox and Mrs Cox), Mr Hawthorne told her that the white hat seemed just a little ridiculous but was utterly charming and really enhanced the eyes especially if worn low, so that the eyebrows, if not completely obscured, allowed just the smallest shading of fine dark lines to be seen. And then there was the pene-trating green-eyed look (the green taken up from the partly buttoned overcoat); and then the healthy clear white of the eyes themselves which could startle, with delight, anyone catching her gaze in passing . . .

He was looking at her, as he spoke, as if no one else was in the dining room. She looked at his rather large and serious face and, in her thoughts, began to unpack and hold in both hands the little walks to and from buses or trains, especially when he was seeing her home after class. And then there were the occasional little meals together and the magic pleasure of the music at the concerts. All this they had managed to have together because of his fond and reliable calculated way of making arrangements. She went on allowing herself, in her mind, to see the rather elderly man, sitting opposite, as an obedient little boy being taken to his kindergarten by his Nanny, and then he, aged eight, would have been sent to prep school and on to boarding school at eleven.

And then, at eighteen, to university and on to a commission in the Army, and as the years passed, as a lawyer, called to the Bar, a Barrister, an Advocate, a professional Pleader, a King's Counsel (or a Queen's, depending upon who was sitting on the throne) . . .

He was looking at her and speaking to her gently, drawing her out from her thoughts, the last being the restrained passion and the tenderness in their embrace on the little footbridge. He was explaining about the Tribunals in London and how people would have the chance to explain their beliefs and attitudes . . . He was not sure about the length of time he would have to be away, maybe several months. Wartime was like that, he said in his kind way.

She, trying not to cry, told him she wanted to go with him, to be with him. She said she knew the war caused grief and uncertainty. She told him that she could not live without him. 'I want to be with you,' she told him.

'I want to be with you, too.' His voice, speaking to her softly, like a poem or a cradle song, told her it was not possible for her to come with him, *quand même*, not possible, he meant it, he said, 'I shall never forget you, *you – qui remplit mon coeur de clarté.*'

The visit to Mr Hawthorne in Chambers was not so difficult. The mother (Muriel) going up in the old-fashioned cage of a lift wanted the children to behave well. She was herself nervous and she hoped she would not cry or say something silly and ruin the visit. But how could a visit to Mr Hawthorne be ruined. He would, at once, see that it wasn't.

The husband, Henry, had squashed her rather, and 'the relationship', recently by arguing that her feelings for Mr Hawthorne were most likely to be adolescent pre-sexual feelings. In her bereaved state she allowed herself to believe all that Henry said. Though she later thought he might be wrong. It was true that Mr Hawthorne had never given the slightest indication that he was crazy to take her to bed. And she, while allowing herself the deliciousness of a strong manly person as her companion, liked being held and kissed by him. He was capable of great restraint and, because she realised this, she did not in any way suggest a change in their physical behaviour. His kisses were loving and passionate enough to give that excitement and pleasure of each one knowing and recognising desire in the other. She thought often during their times together (not being a stranger to it) of what it might be like to be loved completely to the moment of climax and the warmth of satisfaction. She was not able to know whether in his feelings of desire he preferred to remain perfectly in control and not to abandon himself to something in which control is given up completely, if briefly. She did not raise the subject, thinking that he would perform differently (if he wanted to), or speak of it, if he felt it right to speak at the time.

The little girls took off their raincoats and displayed themselves in their new dresses, dressmaker dresses, which were a present from Mr Hawthorne. They showed him their new outdoor shoes, also a present from Mr Hawthorne. A little maid in a black dress with a little

white apron and a pretty white cap brought in a tea tray.
Mr Hawthorne cleared a space on his desk, and put a
chair alongside his for Muriel. He suggested that Muriel
should pour the tea.

'I am afraid the cake in the tin is rather dry,' he said.
But the little girls, enchanted by the eccentricity of the
rooms, declared that they liked dry cake best. Mr Hawthorne found some new pencils in the desk and shared
them among his guests. Stroking Muriel's hand and lifting it to his lips, he explained about his visit to London.
Sitting on Tribunals was rather repetitive but, he said, it
was worthwhile. Men, he explained, who, in complete
truth, feel that it is wrong to kill other men will have
their attitudes examined and some will be exempt from
active service.

The mother, Muriel, comforted by his gentle caress,
rested and allowed herself to feel happy in Mr Hawthorne's presence. She would remember forever how
he looked and what he said. She noticed his expensive
gold-nibbed fountain pen. It rested in a little tray with
rounded inkwells, like small perfect breasts at either end.

She looked at the books and at the dust and the untidi-ness, resolving to keep him and his rooms in her mind to think about frequently.

Mr Hawthorne, at the end of the visit, came down in the rickety lift with them in order to call a taxi to take them home as the rain had started again and the sky was dark with heavy clouds.

$\mathcal{I}$t was soon after the visit to Mr Hawthorne's rooms that the Police Inspector asked the father if the little girls could take part in an identification parade. The father refused at first and then, reluctantly, agreed for the little girls to look at the photographs.

'All they have to do is to pick a photograph of someone they might have seen in this street or the fields and nearby streets,' the Police Inspector explained, saying that it was on record that the little girls were often out and about here and might recognise a photograph.

'Do you understand?' the father asked them. He told them to look at the photographs slowly and, if there was no familiar face, to say so. But there might be one they recognised.

'What sort of person?' The elder sister looked worried beyond her age. 'We haven't lived here very long,' she said.

'Hush, Lovey,' the Inspector said. The photographs were spread out along the low wall in front of the house.

'You don't have to do this if you don't want to,' the father said as they moved slowly, picking up the pictures which, because of all being in sepia to begin with, looked alike.

'Oh, this one of course!' Suddenly the elder sister, with a cry, swooped on a photograph and waved it for the younger sister to see. Both were excited and pleased to have found a picture.

'It's Victor. We were looking for birds' nests with him.' The elder sister flapped the photograph for her younger sister to see.

'Any more?' the Inspector asked the elder sister.

'Nope,' she said, 'no more.'

'Bit late for birds' nests, isn't it,' the Inspector said. He explained that birds make their nests and lay their eggs in spring and by the end of the summer they're all away. Summer's over.

The Inspector put the photographs away, saying thank you and wishing the little family 'a good afternoon'.

'Oh, Daddy!' The elder sister was trying to look across to the town drain, the footbridge and the fields. She was trying to look at her father and her little sister and at the disappearing shape of the Inspector as he walked up the street. All this she was trying to see through eyes welling and overflowing with tears. The tears came so quickly she looked like a blind person groping for a chair or a table or for a mother or a father.

'Daddy, I didn't mean to give them Victor,' she sobbed. 'Victor was so nice to us. I've given him away. What have I done, Daddy?' She cried. She pressed against his waistcoat while he tried to find a handkerchief with his free hand.

Remembering that Mr Hawthorne had already left for London, the father reminded them that their mother would be home directly. They must hang up the blackout curtains.

'There's a war on,' their father said with indignant sounds in his speech. 'Who's going to set the table and who's going to put the kettle on? First one indoors is the winner!'

Suddenly the father felt terribly alone. A small man has to raise a laugh in a difficult moment in a meeting or at the dinner table. A small doctor might have to stand on a little stool to examine a tall woman's throat. He, the father, on a wet day, cooking out of doors for a picnic in the rain, with a sugar bag over his head and with the fire almost out, the wet black sticks falling apart, he is the one who would be trying to think of something funny to say.

Mr Hawthorne would already be settled in London. Henry could imagine his quiet authority and fair-minded attitude. He felt the sadness which he could not take away from Muriel. He was doubtful about his own attitude and behaviour. Wanting to please and respect Muriel, he had given what could be looked upon as an exaggeration of freedom. This freedom was, he thought, written into their marriage. He loved Muriel and he liked and approved of Mr Hawthorne. Perhaps he had allowed too much freedom, but how can feelings and freedom be measured so that he would be able to say how much freedom he would be prepared to allow. In any case, Mr Hawthorne, several years older than Henry, would not trample on their marriage and take advantage of Henry's generosity. Muriel also, she would never discard the love and the ideals which belonged in their lives together. All the same she seemed to be completely wrapped up in sorrow and was unable to take from him the comfort and optimism he tried to give her. The house was quiet. Outside it was quiet with the stillness and quietness of a green pond. Even their noisy neighbours had not, for some time, called out any greeting, a joke or an insult. They were silent, wrapped in the rules for civilians and the blackout.

The days were following, one after the other, very quickly. After the declaration of war, it seemed as if there had been a hidden state of war in progress for a long time. The war was evident everywhere in the lives of the ordinary people. The fine autumn days seemed to be racing towards the dark evenings and the cold winds of winter. Air-raid shelters became inevitable meeting places. People who, previously, had never spoken to each other, even while living in the same housing estate or apartment block, greeted each other with fatuous remarks, wry smiles and Christian names.

It seemed, as well, as if there had always been well-built ladies sitting at hurriedly erected trestle tables wherever there were buildings able to contain them. These people, The Food Office, they let it be known that they were the custodians of rationing. These ladies, relishing their positions of knowledge and power, relished, in addition, their superiority. They caused at once, wherever they were housed, the formation of the queue. Lines of people were obliged to wait, endlessly, their turn. There were lines of people waiting where they had never waited before. For example, there would be a queue at the railway station, at the bus stop and at the greengrocer's shop if some oranges or onions or a shipment of bananas had made the journey safely. Henry despised this need for a war to bring about this good-humoured neighbourliness. He declared that the wrong people were making decisions, which would cause more troubles in the future.

Henry wanted Muriel. More than anything he wanted her. The war separated people and divided them and, at the same time, forced people to be closer to each other. Henry really wanted to be alone with Muriel and able to talk to her. She was out late three evenings. Coming in from her classes, she said she simply wanted to go *straight away, straight to bed and to sleep*. That she was sad and worried was clear to Henry. He thought she was worrying, perhaps unnecessarily, about the classes or about a student. It would be something extra to the war. He thought at different times, different things. Possibly it was something intimate and delicate. They always told each other everything. He knew she was keeping something from him.

At the weekend, Sunday afternoon, Henry, as usual, made time for a savage preparation for his writing. He mopped the linoleum in the front bedroom. He folded up clothes and put them away and he put out other clothes for washing. He made the bed with clean sheets. And then, after clearing the dressing-table top, he spread out his pages of poetry. He was interested in the sonnet. He knew that some of Shakespeare's sonnets were written to a young man, thus suggesting that he, Shakespeare, was a homosexual. Henry, unlike most of the people he met, saw nothing wrong with homosexuality. But he objected, he once told Muriel, to the idea that people should feel they had to label their sexuality as jam and pickles (chutney also) are labelled. At the time they had laughed about this.

Muriel and the little girls did not disturb Henry. They practised the Beethoven sonata downstairs. And later, when Muriel rested, the children took their dolls to the fields.

Henry, in a self-conscious way, often joked about his poetry. He frequently tore up all the written pages. This afternoon he spent some time, as usual, in copying out a few lines from Wordsworth as an encouragement for his own work.

ELIZABETH JOLLEY

THE PRELUDE

The mind of man is framed even like the breath
And harmony of music. There is a dark
Invisible workmanship that reconciles
Discordant elements, that make them move
In one society . . .

At once he understood that he would never be able to put something of his own next to a real poet. His own work would appear to be empty and stupid. All the same he copied from a previous page:

The queue forms with more people
in line standing as if together but alone.
Everywhere young men in harsh boots and uniforms,
The called-up men, the conscripts, the mothers'
Tears still wet upon their cheeks –
Crowded in trains from one camp to another.
Bitterly cold and wet in towns and villages
They will meet their superior officers
And ultimately face to face

A moment, a pause
And each will salute the other.

by Henry Bell

Henry, knowing from his own National Service, point-less journeys and bleak arrivals, remembers the emptiness and the apparent need which comes immediately before the officer and the man (the soldier) salute.

Of course, the salute is the reason for which they have been travelling.

In his mind, he told Muriel, explaining that he really preferred, as an example, Wordsworth's long poem 'The Prelude' and that he might dismiss the discipline of the sonnet as being too formal for his own small observations on the war and his own memories from childhood and, in particular, his love for her.

And *in particular* he wanted to tell her that he admired Wordsworth's skill in dwelling in the prose of the poem, recreating vividly scenes from long ago with the landscape being a parallel to the turning point, the rite de passage between right and wrong and the sudden understanding of both. All this from a simple, deeply felt, childhood memory.

Leaving the poetry, Henry stared at himself in the dressing-table mirrors. He was gaunt with unhappiness, but gave himself a sort of smile as he remembered their energetic neighbour who, every day, threatened to do that Mr Albert Hilter. 'I'll get him! I'll do for him I will!'

'Hitler – and it's *Adolf*,' Henry, with patience, corrected her but she persisted with her Mr Hilter till, as Henry had to admit, he became a different sort of man when faced directly by Mrs Tonks and Miss Tonks next door. Mr Hilter will remember forever that all Yoomanbeens was very delicate and precious and there was good reason not to crush any of them either with tanks or aireyplanes.

Muriel slept on towards the end of the afternoon. She was sleeping so soundly Henry thought she might have taken sleeping pills. He hoped not. He wished he could lie now, alongside, close to Muriel. He wished that they could talk together about their sadness, which they would first have to acknowledge. He was the one possessing intimate knowledge. Genius and knowing 'what to say', is a responsible thing and has to be imagined rather as he, on the way to school, either on his bicycle or in the bus, imagines his whole morning and afternoon of teaching (the readings, the discussions, the taking of notes), the illumination he wishes for his boys at school, as if it is all written down, in order, in his head, ready for delivery and response. He thinks that other people will have their methods for offering their experience and knowledge, and the approach to learning, all in shape in the mind. Other people might well have this way of approaching their work. A surgeon, for example, could see, in advance, in his imagination every step in the surgical procedure of a certain operation, so that by the time he is in gown, gloves and mask he has confidence because, step by step, in his imagination, he has just rehearsed the knowledge, the experience all leading to the final stages and ultimate success from the first selection of a surgical instrument to the final one.

Henry still sat staring at different pages which were covered with his thin restless handwriting. He, without being able to help himself, as if his mind was too weak to lessen the wishes of the body, went on talking to the sleeping Muriel, his voice an unattractive low hoarse whisper, saying that he felt experienced enough to talk seriously to her, knowing that she was missing Mr Hawthorne so much. In fact, he felt able to say that they are both missing him and must celebrate this deep realisation with their own expression of love for each other. This fitted perfectly in the imagined picture of their married lives and they could find the wish for each other still so compelling it cannot be pushed aside. In his opinion, he growled, love gives no right of full possession. He assured her, while she slept, they both did allow the other some freedom, though it has to be faced that desire was very strong and lack of desire was untreatable. Desire between two people must be present in both. It is not possible to be attracted completely to both the previous lover and the newcomer. This last was their predicament.

Henry, crouched between the three mirrors of the ugly dressing table, stared at his gaunt face in the shabbiness of the looking glass. Until recently Muriel had been late home from evening classes, her pale face blushing pink and her eyes bright and shining as if she might have been kissed and fondled, made much of, admired and desired, so much so that though the signs were unknown to her, they were touchingly familiar to Henry, who, to his shame now, admitted that he had made use of her aroused state as soon as she fell into bed with him. He was, he growled at his three reflections, deeply ashamed.

Henry knew that he was not a foolish idiot. There were men who were fools, he thought, men who did not know or understand that their wives actually changed in appearance during the various stages of sexual stimulation. The voice became husky and the hair had a shining softness. The skin, especially on the face, the neck and the breasts, took on a special radiance. It was unmistakable.

He smiled his gaunt, 'emaciated', wise smile and shrugged his shoulders at his multiple dressing-table reflections as carelessly as he could.

It had not been difficult to guess Muriel's secret. He went into the bathroom to prepare the bath for her. She always appreciated this thoughtfulness even if the little girls took advantage of the hot water before she could. He went on with his mirror talk, distorted now, in his own little shaving mirror. Women, he knew, liked men to have an evening shave with something fragrant and spicy from a special tube, expensive and reserved for special occasions. It was hard for Muriel. He blew out his cheeks in turn. Just when she was ready to experience the previously unimagined male passion in the arms of a well-bred and affectionate man, who obviously had years of good breeding behind in his existence, the new experience – and this was for himself as well, he not being previously attached to any other person, male or female, right in the face of new and rewardingly possible experience – the war was snatching the opportunity away. The lover, still unknown completely and perhaps *unknowing* in his

unblemished innocence, has been 'posted' to London for
an unknown length of time . . .

Henry wanted, at once, to wake Muriel to press himself
close to her in his moments of enlightenment, and to have
once more her sweet response. He would himself be kind
and slow, restrained, calm and powerful. He would blame
himself, put himself in the wrong. He would admit to
being boring, predictable and inadequate in comparison
with the newcomer. He would not even seem to know who
this newcomer was. But, he would be completely tender
and understanding of the whole situation. He believed
fully in her and in himself . . . And with this belief being
uppermost, he tried to think of something ridiculous to say
as she came into the room. Did Muriel know, he asked
from his dressing-table perch, had Muriel *heard* that the
Ration Book Ladies, the doyennes of the coupons, the
Food Office Personnel, they, the inhabitants of the church
halls, now wore those big knickers, the *Directoire* as in
French dressmaking in the seventeenth century. A new

knicker with a substantial gusset and the extra foot in length to the knee. Seriously, he explained that the Ladies had been issued with three pairs each, one pair on, one pair off and one pair in the wash. Same as the Army girls but *they* had to wear khaki. The Food Office had the choice of three colours – peach, lemon or mustard . . .

The trouble in the house, one of the troubles, was that the two bedrooms, because of having a little girl in each room, belonged to all four, Henry and Muriel and the two little girls.

Sundays, as always, Henry wanted to write and study, so he cleaned and tidied one of the bedrooms and made the bed. He seemed to need external order before he could read over what he had written. He spread his pages on the cleared space on the dressing table. He never complained about lack of space, he simply made some cleared place wherever he could see the possibility.

Unlike Muriel, who often walked in the adjoining high-class suburb, wishing for a larger and more gracious house, he seemed to look upon their small house, unmistakably part of the estate, as though it was, actually, what they had always wanted. He always spoke to Mrs Tonks and her daughter as if they were friends, often laughing heartily with them about something, whereas Muriel, without being unkind or rude, would have preferred not to know them.

Theirs was a mixed neighbourhood, Henry often made the declaration, and they should make the best of it.

'Daddy makes a lesson out of everything,' the children came, complaining, back from their walk with Henry, who, anxious to have a little time to himself, had hurried them through the names of the different trees and bushes which made the hedges for the three fields. He had taken the girls riding earlier in the morning, having made an arrangement with the owner of the milk horse. The milk cart came earlier than usual, leaving the horse free from nine o'clock.

Because of her usual routine the milk horse kept

stopping, the children complained when they came home.
The horse, trying to enter one gateway, was stuck, Henry
explained to Muriel and her mother who was visiting for
Sunday dinner (invited). Muriel's mother declared that
she was not amused. The children, in her opinion, could
be, and would most likely be, crippled for life.

Muriel told Henry she would call him when dinner
was ready. He went upstairs, three at a time.

For Muriel the weekends were tedious and dull, the
only prospect being a headache after her mother had
gone. She found herself wanting to talk about Mr Hawthorne. She felt sure something would prevent them,
herself and Henry, from ever seeing Mr Hawthorne again.
She imagined him meeting a society type of lady and
marrying her. She felt depressed and, near to crying, she
forced herself to turn the small piece of meat and the grey
potatoes which she had put in the oven earlier. If only
Mr H. would surprise them with a visit.

The war, the progress of the war, made everything so
uncertain. The Sunday visit from her mother made the
day seem even longer. Her mother never failed to remind

her of her foolish marriage. There was nothing wrong exactly with *Ectore* but only compare him with Mr Hawthorne and see what a difference there was. And Muriel, feeling in her pocket for a handkerchief, wished so much that Mr Hawthorne was coming; she went and opened the front door. No one was standing and smiling out there. She told her mother in a half-whisper that she really did not know either of the two men.

The mother-and-daughter conversation was interrupted frequently by Muriel's mother calling out to the girls while they were practising their piano duet. She could tell, she called to them, that they were not lifting their wrists. And, she added, the loud pedal was not needed. *Noch einmal*, she called again. She wanted them to look at the music sheet. 'What does it tell you there? *Forte* or *pianissimo*? Look!' she screamed. 'You must use your eyes and your brains. You naughty stupid girls!'

Muriel wanted to remind her mother that the girls were still very little girls and were well ahead with their music and languages. Her mother, after stringing the beans, pushed them across to Muriel. She sighed and said she was sorry. It was really because she worried about Muriel being married to a *poète manqué* . . . 'Ectore,' she said, would never come near her expectations; *au fond il n'est pas un homme*, and perhaps more clearly, *er ist kein Mensch!*

'Mother gave me a huge inferiority complex,' Muriel told Henry soon after they were married.

'Let me have a bit,' Henry said, 'I never had one.'

'That is just the silly kind of small-man joke that he would admire,' her mother said when it was repeated for her.

Muriel's mother sighed a great deal. She declared it was impossible to have a sophisticated conversation as she had to be above the long ears of those precocious children.

As well as all this Muriel was sorry over Henry. She was well aware of his honest efforts to create a loving and happy family. It did not seem fair that he should have to put up with her outspoken mother. If she mentioned this to Henry, he immediately said she was not to worry. Her mother, he said, was very interesting. He really liked the old girl, he said.

Suddenly, during the long drawn-out Sunday dinner,
Muriel thought of Mr Hawthorne's long walk home after
class, or simply to see her home, without a class, when he
was no longer in classes. Sometimes, because of staying on
the footbridge for a long time, really only a few minutes,
Mr Hawthorne would insist . . . she was not to worry about
him. He was quite all right – it was never too late when
they had the chance to be together for a few minutes . . .

Her mother's visits caused her to remember how her
mother's severe criticism made her lose confidence over
the pronunciation of some German and French words.
She was quietly grateful for the evening classes in these
languages, her confidence was restored in teaching. And,
of course, there was Mr Hawthorne. The greatest gift she
could have without expecting any gift.

Sundays, Henry, who often described himself as the ink
monitor, the page-turner, the entertainer of mothers-in-
law, was, on Sundays, a bit of a poet, with the emphasis
on 'bit'. He was, as well, a scribe, a keeper of the books,

the bills, the accounts, the expenses and the payments, all being recorded with care, in the exercise book which hung at the side of the dressing table together with the small private notebook on the same hook. The weekly pound note was described as 'paid' in the larger book, with a little note explaining that the change from the pound would pay the relatively small account (don't forget there's a war on) from the butcher; the meat ration remaining small and not changed in any way.

The small red notebook, twirling on its twisted cord, was a small calendar with pictures of flowers and fruits, pet rabbits, cats and dogs, in which Henry recorded what he looked upon as Muriel's secret inner life. Page after page of Henry's small 'legal' (someone had said once about his writing) handwriting. This was not, he explained to Muriel, that he wanted her to keep from the household-expenses money which she had saved. They must not live meanly he said. The children must be properly fed and clothed and housekeeping money was not to be saved for certain extra things.

It seemed to Henry that Muriel really, in spite of

being a wife and a mother and an excellent teacher . . . Muriel was quite girlish, ungrown-up, was a better way of saying it. She was innocent, naïve and even a little stupid about her 'times of the month', her phrase which he adopted, because she was shy about the whole thing and the phrase seemed to hold the actual monthly happening in abeyance. Unless he reminded her from his carefully kept records of dates and calculation of weeks and times, she would be, in her phrase, taken short every time, completely unprepared, angry and 'put out', crying and wailing that she was flooding everywhere.

Henry imagined easily how it might be with a houseful of daughters all behaving in this way all with different days. And, what about a girls' boarding school? He had it in mind to write a successful novel with this theme prominently mentioned on the book jacket. The idea of the simultaneous chaos excited him, but he kept this to himself. He never thought of trapping the monthly miracle in a poem. Rather he felt let down when it seemed that women writers wrote about the onset of menstruation, themselves taking an unfair advantage over the real poets, the men. The writers spent too much time on the loss of blood and did not seem to understand anything of the miracle of a promised life or the waste of a whole army of unused lives.

Since Muriel only remembered when he read aloud the appropriate entry in the notebook, Henry found himself repeatedly at the chemist's shop buying the necessary items, using their trade name as a way of asking for them. This seemed to him to be an academic approach, which was acknowledged by the package being handed across the counter in an anonymous brown paper bag with the thoughtful verbal reminder to save and fold the brown paper because, 'what with the war and one thing and another, there'll soon be no paper bags'.

Henry sometimes read through the little notebooks. If someone writing an article for an emancipated sort of magazine wanted things like 'the serious-minded sex kitten' or 'how many times a night do you have sex?' or 'how many headaches are there in your marriage?' Henry felt that he would be able to furnish a whole series of dates, successes and failures, manifestations of gender preference and difficulty. He would be able to supply, perhaps, an entirely new 'lifestyle' of homage and tolerance, perhaps a 'true story' article which might enlighten the unenlightened, something like 'I shot my husband in order to marry my brother-in-law . . .' Simultaneous chaos would be a good name and description for his article, if he wrote one.

Sometimes Henry faced his understanding, that he was really missing Mr H. Sunday dinners, when Mr Hawthorne was present, had something magical about them. Part of this was his effect on Muriel. He thought again of a magazine, something fresh to take people's minds off the war. 'Simultaneous Chaos' would be a good title for the subject he had in mind. He meant two beds and four people. Something like that.

$\mathcal{T}$he winter, severe with snow and wounded trains, which did not keep time with the last bus or tram, caused the mother to be very late in coming home. She was so much past the time of arrival that the husband (and father) took a chance to meet her. Leaving the two little girls asleep in bed, and placing a guard in front of the almost-burned-away living-room fire, he let himself out by the front door very quietly. He ran with loping strides up the street in no time at all. He kept up this lightness and pace all the way into town to the railway station. The train, more than two hours late on a twenty-minute journey, had not come through. He was told it was sure to be in directly. From the bend, they said, it was possible to make out, through the fog, the lights of the cautious engine.

The husband, Henry, feeling in his pockets, found some unexpected money. He went to the front of the station where a solitary taxi cab and a sleeping driver, snoring, waited. The train was approaching.

Better not to book him, the driver roused himself speaking of himself in the third person. He said to look in the mist where there was a tram kept there for the late train arrival. Of course, he explained, with trams you could only travel on the tram lines and these might not match with the place where you lived. He said it was worth a try because of saving money and perhaps people's lives. He was, he insisted, in no shape whatever to take any passengers. Old and cold, he was in no shape to drive. 'Better off in the tram, all of you, all two of you . . . however many of you there are . . .'

Protecting Muriel, with his arm round her, Henry told her he had been found unacceptable by the ancient taxi driver. And, bent double with laughter, they climbed into the darkened tram.

'Soon be home,' Henry said, putting one arm round the back of her once again. He said he could feel her shivering, a kind of intimate excitement between them.

Muriel, the wife and mother, did not expect to receive any letters from Mr Hawthorne. They had no discussion, prior to his departure, about the possibilities of any correspondence. Since his departure there were times when she wished for a letter from him or that she might relax and sit down and write to tell him how much she was missing him. There was no suggestion that he would be comforted by a letter from her. She often thought how he might have wished to describe his work to her, to give a picture in words of the Conscientious Objectors' Tribunals.

When the letter came in the post that morning telling her about a production of *Fidelio* which was 'going ahead' (Mr Hawthorne's phrase), in spite of the war and in spite of the opera being so long and very 'German', she did not cry and exclaim to Henry about the letter. Simply she pushed it in to her briefcase for reading later, when she would be alone.

She heard with excitement and pleasure the longed-for voice in the words of the short and rather formal, but handwritten, letter. He wanted to know if there was the chance that she could come up to London, at his expense of course, train fares, hotel *und so weiter*. He would be, he wrote, very very pleased to have her company on this special occasion, this long-awaited performance.

She continued to keep her excitement and relief over the arrival of the letter to herself. And, while Henry was raking up the embers and adding small bits of firewood and coal to remake the fire to warm her, she allowed her pleasure over the letter to seem to be entirely over the coaxing of the welcome little flames, and the even more welcome cup of hot milk Henry prepared for her. The milk, like the morning tea in bed, belonged to Henry's gratitude for the way in which Muriel had taken over the evening classes to relieve his over-ambitious teaching programme. He really did feel guilty, he told her, because she was with the children all day teaching *them* success-fully. He sat close to her and kissed her neck.

'Coo-ee *Downright Rotter of the worst sort and thought* . . .

him thinking he's the Bee's Knees, the scandarl the Lov-Lov-Lover Boy...' the melodious voice of neighbour-lady number one rang out in the darkness. Another window was pushed up, the night filling with amber and rose-tinted electric lamps. Neighbour-daughter joined in with a list of crimes and punishments on religious postcards with illuminated texts. 'Holy pictures to be taken down into Hell Fire by Henry Bell Sugar Boy when yas coming over?'

Henry pulled the blackout curtain to one side and laughed, his voice carrying across the black expanse of unfinished roads and houses. He could see the costume jewels and the artificial hair colouring.

'Hey there! I'm coming over!' Muriel heard him shout.

It seemed to Muriel that these two colourful and rather, in her words, awful women were creating a character for Henry, rather like the *life lie* used by dramatists on the stage and by doctors for the man in the street. They were reminiscent, as well, of the idea of the Greek chorus especially when they danced, simply bending at the knees, their voices, in chanted sequence, humming like a swarm of bees, relating violent happenings elsewhere to bring the present time and place into the story . . . accidents, mistakes, opinions and other news.

Henry was soon back. He washed the transmitted facial expressions off and dried himself on the kitchen towel. It was fortunate that Henry could deal with these two women; *street ladies* in Muriel's interpretation.

'I kissed them goodnight,' he told Muriel. It was something to bolster Henry, she thought. And for herself, she had her letter.

The little run in the night had done Henry good. Leaning over Muriel, he put his cold face close to her warmed neck. He had moved the children, he told her, into the back bedroom and they were asleep. He told her to come on up to bed. He would soon warm her up, he said. 'Just see if I don't.'

On the days when Muriel had the evening classes she often woke early. 'Just when I need the extra sleep,' she would complain in a thin, petulant voice, trying not to wake Henry and, at the same time, succeeding in causing him to roll out of the most comfortable side of the bed and to go, as if blind still with sleep, to make tea for them both.

Muriel longed for tea after her sleepless night. In any case, she liked to have tea in bed. Brought up to be frugal, they both enjoyed the unmistakable luxury of the tea tray balanced between them. Muriel, in particular, felt with extra pleasure the contrast between the hot tea and the fresh coldness of linen sheets. The sheets were a present from her mother, for who but her mother had money for best-quality linen.

Henry, unable to find biscuits, came with the tea. Muriel remembered there were no biscuits. The grocer had apologised, his quota had not been delivered. She thought of his kind and solemn face. She knew he was really sorry if there were no biscuits or tinned fruit or an extra strip of bacon – or a tiny bit more cheese for his regular customers – he being the sole keeper of their ration books after the meat coupons had been carefully cut out by the butcher.

When she was in the draper's shop, at the manchester counter, buying the sheets with the gift of money stuffed in her purse, the manageress put other sheets in front of her, something cheaper which would endure forever, didn't need ironing either *and* all in such pretty colours. Yes, it was a synthetic material, a bit like artificial silk . . . But Muriel pushed them aside for the really good quality of the linen.

'You could have had yourself a pretty nightdress or a princess slip with the difference,' the manageress said in an accusing tone, offended that her wholesome advice was rejected.

'I wonder if Mr Gentleman has early-morning tea brought to him by a lover.' Henry was pouring more tea for her, guilt tea, like the hot milk at night. Muriel did not want him to feel guilty. She felt she was the guilty one as she remembered her thoughts during the night.

'I expect Miss Morton brings his tea.' Muriel was pleased to talk about Mr Hawthorne. She wanted to say something ridiculous like suggesting that Henry should hop on to his bike with the teapot. But she had seen something of Henry's awe in the presence of Mr H. When listening to their visitor once or twice, Muriel had seen Henry listening as if completely enchanted as he quietly considered the older man's opinion on some detail to do with the law. She told Henry of the missed frilly nightdress because of the price of linen. He told her he liked the sheets very much and preferred her without a nightdress. She could have the bathroom first, he said.

Muriel, dressing herself quickly, did not want to cause Henry to be late at school. Looking at Henry while he served the little girls with their porridge, she thought how tender and relaxed he was. He was never ashamed to show tender gratitude just as he was always able to show his anger over some hurtful action or bad behaviour. He had allowed the children to look at their comics while they had breakfast.

Because Henry's class was a large class of very restless boys, Muriel wondered whether to show him her letter or not. She did not want to cause him to be late. He always wanted the boys to feel chosen for his classes and excursions, *and* he was *showing them* how to be punctual. His thoughts for the day would be interrupted because of the letter. All the same she gave it to him. He read it quickly, drawing her towards himself. The gentle, well-bred invitation was such a reminder of Mr Hawthorne. Muriel turned her face away and Henry saw that she was crying. He sent the little girls to tidy the bedroom.

'Mr Hawthorne did not write this note to make you cry,' Henry said. He pulled her gently on to his lap. He told her to dry her eyes and to remember how much loved she was. He offered to stay at home. He said that the whole trouble was that she was loved by two men. 'Mr Hawthorne and I, we are stupid enough to love the same woman. This is not the same thing as a married woman carrying on an affair and deceiving her husband, her children and, perhaps, even the lover.' He went on, he told her there was nothing to worry about. He did not want Mr H. or her to be hurt. He said she must write a note to accept the invitation. She must make a list of things to pack. She must . . .

Muriel listened to Henry. She thought of her droopy grey dress. A safe, boring, good quality dress, an expensive gift from her mother, crêpe, almost transparent, showing her shoulder and collarbones, the skirt falling uneasily round her ankles. She dried her eyes. 'Make a list,' Henry said again, 'and pack your case and write a note to thank him. *Fidelio*,' he said. 'Isn't that Beethoven's political theme woven from faith and truth and freedom? And,' he went on, 'the husband is dying slowly because of his integrity, his beliefs, wrongly imprisoned, in a terrible dungeon, deep in the earth and the rocks and then Leonore, disguised as a young man,

arrives just in time to rescue him. I know there's more to
it than that, the descent to the dungeon and Florestan's
unforgettable cry,' Henry paused, 'the voice of despair,'
he went on, 'the hope as he calls her name, not knowing
that she is there. The music is full of partly remembered
pictures,' he said, 'with all the details . . . including the
trickle of water which he is unable to reach. But it is his
crying out of her name which is remembered forever.'
Henry, dressed now, was ready to leave. He gave a short
laugh, a laugh of embarrassment, Muriel thought, as if
he was trying to explain what real love was. A woman, he
told her, is often loved by more than one lover and, it
used to be said or agreed upon, that she ignored all the
lovers except the real one.

'A woman,' he said softly, in the kitchen doorway,
'loved by two men and neither of them can give up their
love for her.' Henry seemed suddenly to understand and,
at the same time, was not able to understand. He was,
Muriel could see, simply swept up, as she was, by something which could make them both feel powerless.

Muriel tried to seem grateful. She was ashamed and

worried about her pretence during the night. Henry was sure to have noticed and was probably hiding a sadness, perhaps even blaming himself. He put an arm round her shoulders and told her that he *would be afraid for her*, but she must remember that Mr H. would never say or do anything which could harm her, so therefore he was *not* afraid.

Muriel tried to follow his thought and words, but all she could feel was fear that Henry would suddenly discover for himself all that was hidden in her. The devastation of a confrontation just before Henry's class at school would be an extra trial. She knew the difficulties in the disturbed behaviour of some of the boys. Henry often came home pale and exhausted.

'Dearest Muriel,' Henry spoke firmly, telling her that she must go to London to Mr Hawthorne and *Fidelio*. He said that she must go with his unrestrained blessings, otherwise Mr H. will not have the company he wishes to have for the special occasion. Henry, as if pleading the case for Mr Hawthorne, kissed her cheek and her hair and, in a mischievous way, her neck, as he said, simply for the immediate response. It seemed to Muriel as if he wanted and could share his ardour with Mr Hawthorne and herself. And his immediate 'lesson' when *Fidelio* was mentioned was so like Henry, the teacher, healing himself before being wounded.

'*Fidus Achet'es* or however it should be pronounced,' he gave a shy little laugh. 'You must be his devoted follower and go bravely in the train to London. He will meet the train. I am sure of that even though there's a war on, he will meet you and take you to your hotel.' He had no fears, he told her, about her safety and her happiness. Embracing her once more, he told her to come out and see him off.

He was up the rough street, on his bicycle in no time. He was late, Muriel knew he could not bear being late, something he hated was to have his ordered mind disturbed.

He should be the one to go to London, Muriel told herself as she went indoors. He understands the opera better than anyone, she wanted to tell Mr Hawthorne, Henry was the one who should be going to the opera. She wiped the stove with a damp cloth and was about to go upstairs to the girls . . .

'I'm late!' Henry was back in the kitchen. He had for-gotten his little schoolcase, he told her. 'I'll think of you all day,' he said, 'and we can talk London and *Fidelio* this evening.'

'I have a class,' Muriel reminded, 'remember?'

'In bed after class then,' Henry said, trying to loop his case to the bicycle with some frayed string. 'Go and walk on the common,' he said. 'Forget lessons for today.' As if suddenly aware of her, Henry told her she looked pale.

'Fresh air,' he said, 'fresh unbreathed air, take the children for a walk. *Fidelio* at bedtime.' He paused and she saw, not for the first time, the concern he felt over her in his clear blue-grey eyes.

It seemed to Muriel that Henry wanted almost to share her with Mr Hawthorne so that Mr H. would be rewarded in the best way possible in a calm, well-bred, intellectual sort of friendship. The kind of thing the ancient Greeks must have had in their literary meetings and writings (when they weren't killing themselves or each other). Henry's enormous respect for Mr H. was another thing, *and*, Henry was not at all 'put out' when Mr H. paid for clothes, pretty clothes, for the girls. Henry seemed to want to give her much more freedom than she had hoped for. Or was he forcing himself and would come down on her and even on Mr H. with misgivings and hurtful recriminations? Henry relied on his ability to heal himself. He must, in his life, have had many occasions when he needed the specific herb of self-healing.

Theirs was a mixed neighbourhood, Henry explained to Muriel, not for the first time. Theirs was a mixed neighbourhood where newspaper boys from the housing estate ran errands, in the evenings, for the rich widows living in the leafy-green, well-watered, well-established ancient suburb.

Elementary-school teachers, he went on to explain,

rubbed shoulders with lawyers, surgeons and self-styled successful business executives.

'You should go out more during the day,' Henry told Muriel. 'You should take the children for walks. A casual meeting in an afternoon might help you to find a friend.' He went on to say that the girls should have riding lessons; 'they cost only seven and six an hour.' Muriel pointed out that for the three of them, herself included, it would be three times seven and sixpence, and as they couldn't, all three, sit on the same horse, it would cost too much. She did not think her mother would agree about the riding lessons, as she could not be relied upon to pay for something not chosen by herself.

Henry, impatient but not wanting to show his impatience, hurried up to the back bedroom where he intended to write for an hour or two. His daily work made him long for the cleared dressing-table top where he could spread out his pages and read them and rewrite them. He understood from his own need for emotional renewal how much Mr Hawthorne, with the stress of his work, needed rest.

Mr Hawthorne had his tennis and his foursome at cards (Bridge), as well as the enlightenment of reading; in London, of course, he did not have the pleasure of the evening classes, but there had been talk of these being closed because of the war and people were not to be encouraged to be away from their homes at night. But then there was music, wireless and gramophone; music was vocational either in composing, in performance or in listening. Music required an intellectual approach as did the reading of poetry and drama and certain books of non-fiction, as well as the various kinds of fiction.

A surgeon learning and developing his operative technique could be seen in parallel with the musician learning to listen, to compose and perform. And, even more than this, was the carrying of the different skills in the memory, this being applicable in the future or sometimes more immediately.

It was the combination of the mind and the movement and the memory, all of it enlivened, animated by the full force of the imagination and by desire. It was a learnéd and a sensory approach, which lifted the creator

99

beyond the ordinary and into the realm of distinction. At such times, and with such thoughts forming within him, the act of writing or trying to write became for Henry irresistible, especially when he seemed to be coming upon an explanation which led to the stumbling on to the one thing which, on some profound aesthetic level, made him happy. He read somewhere that neurosurgeons are highly musical, artistic and imaginative. This gave him immense pleasure. It fitted with the idea that the origin of genius is in the imagination.

Henry did not want to presume that he was on the same level, in any way, with Mr Hawthorne, especially over the need for complete creative relaxation because they each were engaged in stressful work. But it did seem that loving Muriel, to be in love with Muriel, was needed by both himself and Mr H. Surprised at the abbreviation which was a drop into the familiar (unexpected), he sat for some time at the dressing table and ignored his reflections distorted in the three mirrors.

For Mr Hawthorne, being at the opera with Muriel, would provide the necessary relaxation for him. And it was not difficult to understand that, for Muriel, the journey to London, and to the opera with Mr Hawthorne, would be an unexpected and therefore even greater enrichment.

With all this suggestion of benefit, it seemed to Henry nothing – there could be nothing wrong with the proposed arrangements. He sat on scribbling a few notes on the poignant urgency of Florestan's cry from the depths of rock and despair, the tenderness, in contrast, of the quartet 'Mir ist so wunderbar', and the subdued gratitude for fresh air and sunlight in the prisoners' chorus.

To be at the opera with Mr Hawthorne, to be close beside him, listening to the music, knowing that he had wanted her to come as his companion would, Muriel thought, be the sweetest pleasure, sweeter than anything earlier during her life.

Warm in bed, the previous night, in the darkness, like a blind person, gently and secretly, feeling with her hands her husband's thin but strong body, in particular his chest rising and falling as he breathed in sleep. Resting her head on the regular movement of his reliable chest, she allowed herself complete happiness, the anticipated happiness of travelling up to London, invited by Mr Hawthorne especially to accompany him to the opera and to stay in London, in an hotel, overnight. Being at the opera with Mr Hawthorne, close to him, beside him, listening to the music while he was listening to it and knowing that he had wanted her to be there with him was *really* the sweetest thing to happen in her life. She had to understand, at the same time, that there really could not be a suggestion of any intimate nakedness between them, herself and Mr Hawthorne. She felt unable to tell Henry, to discuss her feelings with him. If anything was said, Henry would be adamant that Mr Hawthorne was so much a gentleman, and as such was innocent, so much so that it would be stupid and degrading to even think, in that way, about him. To console herself she, taking on Henry's way of speaking and pretending, told herself to simply imagine Mr Hawthorne in a Turkish Bath where the rising steam would caress and hide the body rather like a thick white-lace curtain. That would be Henry's way – to bring in an entirely different image. She whispered to the sleeping chest that she wanted, more than anything, to sleep and to wake up without her present worries.

Sometimes when I'm in a train I get to feeling really randy, her college friend said once. *Embarrassing*, she confided, *and so lonely and squalid to end up in the toilet, so wasteful, utterly wasteful . . .*

Muriel was never able to forget Leonie's apparently lightly spoken confession, even now when she never saw her friend and did not know, or care, where she lived and what she might be doing.

Travelling by train was something she enjoyed. She tried to put Leonie out of her thoughts but, instead, remembered another one-sided conversation which could spoil the wished-for forthcoming journey.

Once you pretend, Leonie said on this other occasion, *once you pretend, you know, because you can't make it because of wanting someone else or because of some other reasons, so you, as the Americans would say, you fake it. Well, the whole thing becomes just that – a fake, a pretence, a repetitive fake, self-conscious and it's impossible to get back to the real thing. And the hardest part is the jealousy of happiness in other people.*

Muriel remembered clearly the unwanted conversation, Leonie persisting with it and giving the information which was frightening and depressing. The sleepless night seemed endless.

And the man, Leonie said at the time, *the man always knows the fake. Men can feel it and they never say anything about it but you do see, don't you, Mu, that it can never be the same again. A man can feel the pretence the whole goddamn thing even when there isn't even a pinch of jealousy in him . . .*

Henry, Muriel faced the thought, Henry would not put up with any pretending. On the other hand, he would *know* and, in a fair-minded way, would be sure to say, kindly, that he could feel the difference. Or, she had to finish the thought, he might imprison himself in the silence of unwanted knowledge.

In the misleading warmth and spring-like fragrance of the heath Muriel let her thoughts, once again, dwell on happiness to come. She had been stupidly anxious during the night, keeping herself awake with ugly thoughts till Henry, waking, disturbed by her sobbing, went downstairs to warm some milk for her. On returning and finding that she had fallen asleep, he drank the milk himself and, creeping into bed as smoothly as possible, he gathered her to himself, holding her tenderly while she slept.

The two little girls were like two little dogs running excitedly on the common. The mother, Muriel, cautioned them to stay near her and explained that the immense pylons were needed to carry electricity to people and to factories. She tried to make a little afternoon class out of the pylons. 'And what do we want electricity for?' she asked. But the little girls disappeared laughing in the bracken and behind the gorse bushes. Muriel remembered expressing distaste for the pylons, these monstrous 'creatures' stepping out it seemed not simply to reach the housing estates but as if to

girdle the earth with ugliness. Henry, on that earlier occasion, told her or rather gently reminded her that she was
pleased to have electricity in her house so it was likely that
others would share this wish, to say nothing about all the
other uses for electricity.

Muriel was glad that she had brought the children to
the common. They, for their afternoon class, acquitted
themselves in mental arithmetic and spelling during the
short bus journey. An elderly passenger, during their
spelling, clapped his hands at their success with 'ambitious' and 'matrimonial'.

Muriel felt the air, the fresh air, caressing her face and
neck. She sighed and sat down on a patch of short rough
grass. A few sheep came and looked at her and she could
hear the happy voices of the children nearby.

Beethoven wrote only one opera. She wanted to tell Mr
Hawthorne even though he already knew this. He would
smile that quiet little smile of pleasure as he always did
when she was teaching him something.

In the noble opera the magic is in the music of descent, the unreachable dungeon, a place of suffering and final despair. Florestan's voice, pleading as he calls for Leonore, is heard by the audience as Leonore arrives to rescue him. The audience, in this dramatic development, knows as well that the other prisoners are about to be brought out into the fresh air and the sunlight. Free at last.

It was the quality of drama and sorrow in Florestan's voice which led Muriel, at one time, to speculate on how a man, or perhaps a boy to begin with, first knows that he has a powerful and passionate singing voice. Would he, she wondered on occasion, would he suddenly sing a note, a fine long drawn-out, passion-laden voice in the bathroom, a mature tenor, startling his mother and his father as they paused to listen, respectively (in hair curlers and down-at-heel slippers), attacking their bacon and eggs at the kitchen table. And their immediate neighbour, 'I always said there's sumthin up with that boy. He's a Queer One,' nodding and agreeing with herself out of sight, sucking her teeth and peering under the lifted curtain.

And the boy himself with all the youthful years of

singing with the innocent purity of the boy soprano, after the realisation of the sound, almost like a cry, the boy himself has the responsibility, forever, of protecting the ability to produce this sound. He would discover that the sound came in a mature fullness with the necessary exertion to produce the sustained and perfect note involving his mouth, his throat and his lungs. Really he would have to admit to himself that his whole body and his mind would be taking part in the production of the pure beauty of the special gift.

Muriel thought of the restrained and subdued quality of the prisoners' chorus when they are set free and are able to straighten their bent shoulders in their freedom. She thought of the quartet and the fanfare of trumpets . . . The boy becoming, by means of his voice, a man, might look at himself in the speckled bathroom mirror with unquestionable pity and awe.

Mr Hawthorne, after class one evening when they were waiting for their trains, spoke suddenly, all in a rush as if he felt he should not be saying the words he was saying. He wanted, he said, to say that German was a language which spoke of love. The feelings which people had for each other mattered so much; it was important to have a language which expressed, with a choice of words, a particular deepening of the voice, and an emotional nuance which changed as thoughts changed. The beauty of the language, had she noticed?, he wanted to know, that the voice speaking in German was deepened with tenderness? German speech and music, he said, changed and were charged with suggestion and meaning. The music in *Fidelio* had the same effect, he said. The music and the German language set the imagination free. He longed for complete freedom, he said, holding her close to give her warmth. The platforms were draughty and badly lit and there were no fires in the two waiting rooms. Mr Hawthorne went on to say that he hoped he had not said too much. Of course not, Muriel told him. She was concerned, she said, because he would be so late back to London, taking a later train because of looking after her. He wanted to look after her, he said then. The weather had, he said, been very thoughtful for his wishes. This was the last night of night journeyings they would be doing. The war had seen to that, closing the classes and taking off some trains. He said there was nothing to be done about this.

Their kiss was interrupted by the arrival of the trains, both late. From inside the compartment of her train, Muriel watched and saw him turn slowly to walk to his own train, which had come alongside hers from the opposite direction.

Muriel was grateful for the richness of his restrained and perhaps shy affection. She could, she thought, wait calmly until the time came for her to travel to London as his guest. During the class he had made the illuminating remark that the music in the opera *Fidelio* suggested an affirmation of love and freedom. Leonore, he said, was the symbol of freedom in the rescue of her husband and in bringing about the liberation of the wrongfully imprisoned. He longed for freedom, he said, while he kissed her as the trains steamed in, complete freedom, he said.

Muriel in the bracken, on the common, was not quite calm about going to London and Henry's stout declaration that she must accept the invitation.

Mr Hawthorne was, of course, settled for the time being in London. He was sure to be in an hotel with lawyers, advocates and secretaries. Naturally he would reserve a single room for her in that hotel or in one close by. The Club, his club, was for gentlemen only, she understood that without being told. She thought a single room near to a bathroom would be nice. The luxury of a bathroom to herself was unthinkable.

There was, as well, the fairytale thought that Mr H. would reserve a double room or a suite with white and gold furniture, champagne and flowers. He seemed too shy to reserve anything. In spite of his reticence, Mr Hawthorne would be charming and amusing and he would not hesitate to express himself quietly over the music, the quality of it and the singing and the reactions of the audience. She thought of him possessing a handsome dressing gown, a garment tailor-made for a gentleman. He would be quite at home in the hotel bedroom. He would go out on to the balcony of the room and warn her not to join him, 'much too cold,' he would tell her, coming indoors once more and extinguishing his cigar.

She would wear her own silky dressing gown and move smoothly about the room in the wealth of an atmosphere created by the cigar and the discarding of it with such well-bred nonchalance.

Muriel felt the sudden chill, a small cold wind left behind by the forgetful winter, penetrating her warm coat. It made her realise that she had been taken in by the sunshine which, in reality was weak and fading rapidly. It was very quiet, no sound at all of the children's voices. She was afraid she had fallen asleep there on the deceitfully warm earth. In the silence, as the sky became more overcast, she looked at her watch. Surely she had been sitting there for only ten minutes or so. She began to walk about in a rapid distracted way, running to one gorse bush and then to a patch of bracken and on to another more abundant, a veritable sea of ferns. She ran and stumbled, calling out the children's names in a stupid ineffectual voice, bordering on hysteria and weeping. She ran downhill and came to a fence she did not remember. There were no fences on the common, she knew that, but this was a long efficient fence, in both directions, preventing anyone from going on down into the valley. **W. D. Keep Out**, she saw the notices and realised it was a War Department fence. 'There's a war on,' she told herself.

She hurried breathlessly up the hill, tears flying from her face and her heart thumping. She was afraid something terrible had happened to the children and she thought of their fear. How could she, she added to her pain, how could she have been sitting and daydreaming about Mr H. when her children, unwatched, were in danger. She prayed to a neglected God to help her to find her children and she prayed to have them safe from fear and harm.

She thought she saw a child ahead. Dusk was approaching fast. She thought she could see one of the girls standing and waiting but, as she drew nearer, she saw that it was simply a gorse bush. She ran on hardly able to breathe. She, without meaning to, thought about Henry and how cross he would be. And then she thought of her mother and how, quite rightly, her mother would say what she thought, bringing in Henry for his share of the blame.

What were some of the things her mother said about Henry? She sometimes, absentmindedly, called him Dennis or Hector pronouncing these names in her heavy French accent, especially Hector, *Ectore*. Then usually found fault, with her own reasons, about both names, in spite of neither belonging to her daughter's husband. She then moved on to declare Henry as ambitious in matrimony and, in matrimonial ambition, was educating himself beyond his ultimate position in life. And to add to that, she would say he was bent on educating, on *cramming* her two pretty granddaughters. Left to him, they would turn out to become ugly blue stockings *unwanted by any man*, her mother warned, let alone the handsome prince each child deserved.

'Why do you think I urge these two lovely babies to wash with cold water every morning?' she would ask. 'It is, and you should remember this, it is,' her mother would say, 'for the time when the suitors, the handsome princes will come seeking their brides, wanting to decorate these two beautiful white necks with necklaces of precious stones each one fastened on a fine chain of hand-beaten gold. And another thing,' her mother never kept to one remark . . . there were always more. 'And another thing,' she went on, 'where is their sweet behaviour? I am asking, where?'

'But, Mother,' Muriel gasping for air, stammered, 'Henry insists on pretty clothes for them and he approves of your cold baths. He has one, every day, himself. As for sweet behaviour the girls always sit down and write to you to thank you for presents . . .'

The elder child, as soon as she saw her mother coming out of the darkness, ran to her weeping, saying that she was afraid that she had lost her mother forever. And, as if in a confession, she said she had lost the little sister. 'And I am supposed to take care of her,' her voice came and went in breathless gulps as she tried not to cry.

'We must find her,' Muriel said, taking the child's offered hand. 'She must be somewhere. We'll find her and then all go home together.'

'It's dark,' the child said.

'I know,' Muriel agreed.

'She might have gone to the bus,' the child said.

'Yes,' Muriel tried to agree.

'She might be hiding to jump out on us.'

'She might,' Muriel wished that she would, now, at once. 'Is that what you were playing?'

'Yes, we were going to jump out on you.'

They walked on. 'She might have gone to the bus,' the child said. 'It's quite a long way, but she knows the way.'

Muriel imagined the terror and the fear the small child might be suffering. 'Yes,' she said. 'She might have gone to the bus. Come, let's hurry.'

They held each other tightly by the hand. Muriel thought how easily the child could have been run over crossing the main road, or kidnapped in the dark and lonely hollows in the common. There were accounts, sometimes in the newspaper, of children disappearing.

Muriel was afraid of what Henry might say and do if and when they returned late and drenched in the now heavy rain . . . and one of them missing.

'We'll have to go back once more,' Muriel said when

they reached the main road. 'She's not here.' The child tucked her warm capable hand into the mother's cold hand. They turned back across the heath.

'Daddy won't be cross,' the child said suddenly. 'He's never cross if it's something we couldn't help, like me spilling the milk. He just said the milk shouldn't have been put into the one big jug. That's all he said.'

All the same Muriel was frightened. Henry put up with almost everything but, even for Henry, the loss of the child was unthinkable. Her stupid carelessness was unforgiveable, treacherous. 'Call her. Loud,' Muriel told the elder sister. She, herself, had no voice. She felt strangled in her own thoughts of the little child's fear at being all alone, in the rain and the darkness. Fear had taken all strength from her voice and her body.

They had not walked far when they saw the dark shape, darker than the gross and ugly shapes of the furze bushes. The small figure came bowling towards them, solidly stomping along, head down, with all the determination the younger child of a pair needs to have.

'That's Daddy whistling,' the elder child said. 'Do you

hear him? That's our daddy. *Come to the cook-house door,
boys*, that's his special tune. He whistles for us to come
home, when you're out,' she told her mother. 'When
you're out,' the explanation was more of an accusation,
or so it seemed to Muriel. The child explained to her
mother, 'when you're out, and he's making our baths and
our supper. He whistles for us to come in from the field.'
She paused. 'Mother,' she said, 'this is Victor.'

No need to introduce him, Muriel kept the thought
to herself, he was too well known already. The child was
defensive, Muriel thought, as they left the lane and the
footbridge and were walking alongside the recently
storm-heightened, lively waters of the drain. Muriel tried
to hurry, her clothes were suddenly too heavy.

'This is Victor,' the elder sister explained again to her
mother. 'He's saying he's been looking for us all round the
roads along with Daddy. They even went to the common
but *must have* missed us. He says Daddy's gone back
upstairs to try *Come to the cook-house door* from the back
bedroom window . . . again . . . in case we're lost up in
the new roads and would hear him better.'

'Thank you, Victor.' Muriel, allowing herself to dismiss Victor but remembering her good manners for a moment, enjoyed the comfort which accompanies being well bred, to soothe her dreadfully uneasy mind. How could the children have been so completely lost like that, so absolutely not there and then so gently found as if brought back by someone wearing soft slippers and gloves?

'Say goodnight to Victor,' Muriel told the girls, 'and tell him thank you.'

Surely Victor was not responsible for their temporary but too long absence. Surely, if he had been with them there on the common, they would never have been lost. He seemed to know every stick and stone of the place.

'Where's your Mr Gentleman tonight?' Victor asked. Muriel could see he did not understand that he was being dismissed.

'He's not here.' Muriel, surprised at the sharpness of her own voice and her stupid answer in which she, at once, caused herself to admit to being part of a couple with Mr Hawthorne, cleared her throat and assumed a superior tone.

'Goodnight, Victor. And thank you very much for helping us tonight. Off you go now, *off home*,' as if sending a stray dog home. She sighed, 'I can never understand what that boy says,' she said to the two little girls. 'He sounds queer, like an idiot,' she said, as if able to punish Victor in some way by saying this.

'He's not an idiot,' her elder daughter said with some defiance, 'it's just that he hasn't any roof to his mouth so the words don't come out properly, out of his mouth. You really have to *really* listen.' The two little girls wanted to show their mother Victor's bed. It was like a nest, they said, under the wooden part of the bridge, all lined with grass pulled up and wrapped round, they said. Just like a bird's nest.

'I want to sleep in Victor's bed,' the younger child said. 'I want to go to bed.' She began to cry and hang on to her mother's heavy coat.

All at once they were at their own gate, where Henry took Muriel in his arms telling her it was all his fault. It had been his idea for them to go for a walk. He was sorry, he said.

Muriel, in his embrace, felt her own fear, which began, as relief increased, to be merely an irritation. He was sorry, Henry said it all again, adding that he would never be so thoughtless . . . not ever.

'He's had a dozen or more kittens the night.' A familiar voice screamed enjoyment across the darkness. 'We're having a real good *Schadenfreude* the night, tonight. Lost kiddy night! and lost wife night, oh dear me.'

'Oops, where in hell is my lovebite I was going to show *you*, Dolly.' And Miss Dolly replied, 'Mind the blackout, Ma, you'll have the curtings into the soap dish if you don't look out and a cautionary fine to top it all off.'

'Found your kiddies, have you? And your wife? Some get all the luck. Found all found. 'OORAY!'

'No doubt about you! Found all found and held, you're a good man, Mr Henry Bell.'

At the sound of the voices screaming across the unfinished roads and the empty unfinished houses, Muriel turned to look. In the exposed warm light from the open kitchen door it was possible to look in on the private dressing and undressing. The one-time intimate party clothes and underclothes, the wraps and shawls, were decorated with cheap, imitation jewellery pinned on as if without thought or planning. The cheap beads and imitation gold and silver bracelets caught the forbidden light and sparkled as if challenging the enemy . . . and, of course, ignoring completely, as usual, the rules of the blackout.

'Aw forget your lovebite, Ma, it's almost faded. Talk about having kittens, Ma, talk about twelve kittens in all. But no I tell a lie, three dozen kittens that man's had a night to remember before it was night.'

'Found your ways back then?' Mrs Tonks joined in. 'Found your ways home? There's no place like home!' she bellowed. 'There's no place like home,' she lowered her voice, 'you know, Dolly, he was really upset.' The voice carrying across the evening continued: 'You know, Dolly, I never seen a man that upset and *you know* I seen plenty men in my time, I know 'em inside and outside and it don't ever do to encourage that what's going on here. Give a girl a inch and she'll take a yard. It don't do to be free and easy like. You mark my words, Dolly girl, he has been and was and is real upset and, nice man as he is, he's not going to let it show. You wait!'

Henry said that he would go over to the Tonks and set their minds at rest – but family first, then Tonks.

'Can we have a kitten? Daddy? Can we have one of the kittens? Can we have two? One each. Daddy, one each, can we, please, can we, can we . . . ?' The little girls hung on to Muriel's heavy, wet travelling outfit, a jacket and a skirt made to measure from an Austrian Loden cloth. The sight of which made Henry, all at once, deeply sad. That she had dressed up for the walk somehow made it worse, much much worse.

'Two kittens, Daddy, please,' the voices insisted.

Henry, pulling the children into the house, as if by their ears and their hair, said the kittens were merely a figure of speech and were not available as pets, and would they hush their noise and it was time for their bath. And, as a treat, for being lost and found, he was going to make fried potatoes for them . . . He told them to hurry with the bath because their mother was cold and wet and she needed a nice hot bath as well.

'Daddy, what's a figure of speech and who, Daddy, is Mr Gentleman? Is that you, Mr Gentleman?' Muriel heard the children as they hurried downstairs in their bath towels. She heard them as she ran her bath.

'Daddy, who is Mr Gentleman? Who is he?' She did not hear over the noise of running water what reply came from Henry. From the other house, perched a little higher than theirs, came the sound of singing and then, 'Anyone for tennis? Oops! Anyone for lovebites, oops pardon me . . .' A screeching voice and then silence and darkness as the next-door kitchen door was slammed shut.

Muriel, in the privacy of the bathroom, thought about the children and how they did not miss anything. She thought, as well, how irritating they were when they hung on to her clothes, especially this evening when she was wet through and tired. Victor, she thought, must know all about the long kisses since he was in the fields and the lane and near the footbridge all the time. She felt guilty and miserable about her attitude towards Victor. She took so long over her bath, the water was no longer hot. She was unable to stop thinking about Mr

Hawthorne. She smiled, thinking of the way he had of shyly unbuttoning her long coat in order to be able to draw her closer to himself, without the coat coming between them, as if they were both inside the coat . . . one intense kiss led to another and they clung to each other supporting themselves against the timber of the little bridge. He was always waiting for her on the evenings when she had classes (though it seemed clear that the classes would not survive the war). He so much enjoyed, he said, looking forward to being with her – if only for the short time when he could see her home. She longed so much to see him that she thought she should not make problems over seeing him. Thinking constructively, she would maintain the happiness when Mr Hawthorne returned from London, some time in the future, by getting rid of Victor. She would not harm him, she told herself, just get rid of him. Simple!

Often on her way home from shopping, Muriel walked by the little church on the corner of the main road where a

lesser road, when finished, would cross over. It was a
pretty building with dark roofing tiles, a bell tower and
a spire. Because of the war the bells were silent.

Muriel thought the church was similar to remembered churches in Germany. The substantial double
doors faced west, mellow in the late afternoon sunshine.
A *Church Open* notice was, as a rule, propped against one
of the doors. Muriel often thought she would sit in the
church to rest, with her shopping neatly on the floor
beside her, as Bavarian women, peasant women, might
rest with their bags of vegetables reposing against their
varicosed legs.

Another frequent thought was that she would go to
the Sunday morning service and, taking the little girls,
she would sit where she could see Mr Hawthorne. This
was, of course, before his being in London for the COs
Tribunals.

When she told Henry, at the time, then, of her intention, he reminded her that the church was really a part of
the boundary between a well-established and wealthy
suburb and the unfinished sprawling housing estate

where the landlord came every fortnight to collect the rent from the inhabitants, themselves included. He went on to remind her quickly that, at that church, the congregation was more than just Mr Hawthorne. A great many would be people capable of severe disapproval of anyone who was not 'one of themselves'. And she must know in her heart, she was not 'one of them'. And *she must know in her heart that she was not and could never be like them at all.*

'You don't fit in with these people,' he said. 'You're having Mr H. for Sunday dinner after church, and I'm coming up with a text for discussion every week, *and* the rent's paid, *and* you can gaze at him as much as you like here at the dinner table. Really, Muriel, don't be daft!' Henry said 'daft' with a short vowel, it snapped at her and made her feel sillier than ever.

Lying in bed, not asleep, close to Henry, who had taken extra care to bring her to the edges of desire and, between kisses, telling her that he was audacious, wanting her all over again. He wanted her intensely, he said, and she could moan as much as she liked. Even with all this, *and* his fond laughter, she was not able to respond. And sadly she knew she would not be able to sleep and would be bitter, ugly and petulant in the morning, and for the whole day. She was often aware of her own behaviour and the ways in which Henry suffered and tried to lift her black mood.

She thought again of Mr Hawthorne's description of the organist's graceful and agile movements. He had noticed, as well, the organist's very small feet and that, when he played the hymns, it was as if his whole body and his mind were involved in producing the music. She allowed herself to think once more of Mr Hawthorne's description of the organist while pretending to respond to Henry's audacity (there was nothing he couldn't bring off, he whispered close to her), she let herself feel the entire moment in Mr Hawthorne's stronger and heavier embrace. Henry thanked her in the quick beating of his heart. 'Come closer,' he breathed into her neck, 'let's do that again.'

At times like this Muriel thought that her husband was even more than ever like the quick red-brown nimble fox. 'You need a comma with all those adjectives,' she said in her head as if correcting a student.

All the same she found herself, instead of falling asleep, thinking about and comparing the two men in several different ways. Henry, slim and taut, wearing well-washed corduroy, faded and fraying, in contrast with the aristocratic, she thought, sartorial, slightly perfumed elegance of the older man, Mr Hawthorne.

Mr Hawthorne, obliged to be away in London because of the war, was, for an indefinite time, missing his prepaid evening classes. And he would be lost, she thought, without Miss Morton to look after him. Miss Morton, experienced and fond, had been with him for most of his life. A cherished and cherishing housekeeper.

For as long as she had known Henry, he had worn and been proud of wearing a second-hand Harris tweed jacket which had leather patches on the elbows and leather binding at the wrists. She was not able to avoid remembering how much the jacket comforted her, whenever they were able to meet, during the time when her mother's disapproval almost prevented their marriage. At that time the wish for one of the houses on the estate, the new estate, where the occupants had to be ready with the rent money, was like an impossible dream. The warmth and the strength of the man, Henry, at that time, seemed to be stored in the good quality woollen cloth.

$\mathcal{E}$very time she tried to imagine Mr Hawthorne naked, she was prevented by the reality of his immaculate appearance, his suits, the jackets, the waistcoats and trousers, made to measure by a tailor, from the same kind of cloth, usually a fine quality, dark-coloured worsted, knowing the soft silky linings of the waistcoats would be symbolic of an intimate acquaintanceship. It was unquestionable, he was very reserved. He would be very shy, she thought, and possibly entirely inexperienced, in spite of giving an impression of himself as being quietly competent and complete in every way.

Did his housekeeper, she wondered, did Miss Morton teach him the correct behaviour for various confrontations, and other things, such as which foods and drinks to avoid and, especially, which women might be regarded as bad and harmful sexually? Or was his father, years ago, his mentor? This father, she wondered what he was like, in spite of certain knowledge she had, for example there was the father writing for his son in selected books: Thackeray, Cervantes, Defoe, Dickens and Hardy and others, when he was a schoolboy. She was only able to guess: *For Roderick Hawthorne From Father* followed by a slightly smudged, pale, inked-in date. She tried to imagine then what his naked body might be like, and what expectations he would have about hers. She was silly, she thought, like a schoolgirl. She must have slept then. For, when she woke to daylight and the noisy sparrows on the bedroom windowsill, the family were already washed and dressed, downstairs.

The days and weeks passed slowly. A Sunday and one more Sunday Mr Hawthorne and *Fidelio* not so far off in time. Muriel, an unwilling partner in the Sunday late rising and unfinished love-making (the children having come with silly requests, repeatedly, to the parents' bedside), continued unwillingly with her Sunday morning housework. She pushed a small piece of disagreeable-looking meat and some potatoes into the oven. She was still in her drab dressing gown when a policeman knocked at the front door. He explained that the identity photograph picked out by the girls had proved to be very useful and the young man, a boy really, had been settled with different foster parents. Muriel, at first, did not remember.

'It's Victor,' the children told her after the police officer had gone. Victor keeps the bridge, they explained, but he might have been put somewhere too far away from them now. 'He knows all the birds' nests,' the younger child said. 'I want Victor,' the younger child began to cry.

Muriel was still in her dressing gown, *wishing she could be rid of Victor*, when her mother arrived.

'Muriel!' The mother began straight away to correct the daughter. 'Muriel, you must remember . . . I never let Ernst, I never let Ernst, your farzer, see me with an unwashed morning face. Always I sprinkle myself. Quickly with ice water. Quickly to be fresh for him. I would have been ashamed for him to find me unwashed.'

Henry was out early in order to bring the milk horse round for the girls to have their riding lesson.

Muriel could see Henry's energetic behaviour was meant to help in the entertaining of her mother. She felt grateful and surprised herself by realising that Henry, in his boyish innocence, could be missing Mr Hawthorne. After all it was the two of them, Henry and Mr Hawthorne, who discussed first one text and then another, usually one was the basis for the church service and she imagined the sermon lifting Mr Hawthorne, cradling him from the end of his working week to the beginning of the next week. Mr Hawthorne and Henry had plenty of human troubles, all with their differences, waiting for them after the supposed resting time during the weekend.

Muriel, while making little piles of fresh underwear for her small suitcase, thought with a small slow allowance of pleasure, like a little nibble of chocolate in secret, of Mr Hawthorne. She thought of her mother downstairs in the kitchen and was grateful, in silence, to Henry for having the idea and the sense to buy a Sunday newspaper (a high-class one) while he was out.

'To keep your mamma out of mischief,' he had said before going, as he said, to look over the horse arrangement.

It was too soon to pack but Muriel felt it was a sort of comforting thing to do. Mr Hawthorne, she thought, would *make love*, she disliked the banal phrase, he would *make love* as he played tennis, very determined and not distracted by any incident or person, or any thought. He would concentrate as he had to with his work and, as he chose to, with his tennis.

'Muriel,' her mother's voice interrupted unpleasantly.

'Muriel,' her mother said while Muriel shared the small amount of meat on to the plates. 'Muriel,' she said. '*La douche* is for every day.' Muriel nodded, counting potatoes on another plate.

'*La douche* is for every day,' her mother said. 'You must never present yourself *sans la douche*.' Muriel did remember but, as she told Henry after lunch, when her mother had gone upstairs to have a rest, she did remember; but the damn thing took up so much time. She had three evening

135

classes a week, two for German (Beginners and Advanced)
and one French class (mixed). Three nights out in a row.
She would repeat her difficulties to herself and to Henry.
She would include the train and bus journeys. These took
up so much time. Her voice rose as she reminded herself
and Henry of her hardship. She spoke in a thin high voice,
complaining to herself, her anticipation of pleasure and
her grievances hopelessly mixed. 'I'm sick of the war!'

'La douchesse,' Henry said, pulling Muriel onto his
lap. 'Why let her bother you so? She's having a lovely
nap, I covered her up just now and the girls are playing
their whispering game – so all's quiet. Think about your
London visit. Have you made your list of things to take?
Forget about *la douche*. Think about me,' he said. Muriel
thought about Henry. She thought about him often.

Henry maintained that the human body was largely self-
cleansing. It was not like knives and forks and cups and
dishes, cooking utensils and milk jugs caked with particles of
food in the little ridges or the pinholes which were, he said,
a haven for harmful germs, 'bacteria' was a better word, he
spelled it twice for the little girls when they came downstairs.

Henry never objected to doing the washing-up and the family washing. These were only two of his useful accomplishments. His bad habit was that usually he did not finish household work so the small house often seemed to be hopelessly untidy. He said that if you were doing something else, reading or writing something, then housework became second only to the more important occupations.

Victor was so badly deformed that he scrambled about crouching instead of walking upright. Recently discharged from an institution, Muriel felt that he must be unhappy, perhaps unwanted, in the foster home provided for him. He was frequently in the fields or the back lane and, of course, the footbridge seemed to belong to him. Muriel understood that if he had 'run away' he would have nowhere to go. With some remarkable quality or instinct, he was able to make a place familiar and safe for himself; animal-like in its simplicity of torn-up dried grass and scraps of ragged, torn-up newspaper and material. Victor's nest was completely hidden unless someone approaching, bending double, entered the drain on hands and knees where it flowed under the little bridge.

Muriel begged and prayed, somewhere inside herself, that Victor would like her idea. Much of this idea, she knew, had not been fully thought out. She knew she must feel really sorry for him and try to understand him or else he would come between herself and Mr Hawthorne. And Mr Hawthorne being the kind of gentle gentleman he was, would never be a part of a plan which would cause someone like Victor to be hurt in some way. Her children did not dislike Victor. She could see that he seemed harmless. But she must always remember, she told herself, that he did have that astute understanding which bordered on the shrewd and the crafty. He needed these qualities for survival. Essentially, she felt he was good. She told herself she must not be afraid of him otherwise any carefully organised moments with Mr Hawthorne would be a complete failure. She must be thoughtful and responsible to preserve the delicate feeling between them, herself and

Mr Hawthorne, and Henry and herself *and* Mr Hawthorne. She could not bear to lose Mr Hawthorne and she could not afford to break up her life with Henry.

'Who is that fellow?' Mr Hawthorne might well ask, should Victor be on or about the footbridge at any time.

'Who is that young fellow?' Mr Hawthorne, with a slight movement of his head, as if indicating a possible intruder, might ask.

She would have her answer ready in an easy tone.

'Oh! He's from the other side of the estate, from way out, over there,' with a wide sweep of one arm in a vague direction; 'Over there,' she would reply, 'the roads are not even finished, just the clinkers and gravel. My girls,' she would say, her voice and speech seeming to belong to someone rather dull . . . dull . . . like Henry's sister. It amused her a little to notice with some private shame that, when speaking to Mr Hawthorne, she often tried to distance herself (by suggestion only) from Henry. Henry did not have a sister but *if he did have one*, she argued the point in her mind . . .

Knowing that this was not profitable, Muriel reduced herself at once to a level in which she placed herself alongside Henry and his mythical sister on the too-dull-to-listen-to list. She herself would be incredibly dull, even to the point of being stupid.

How pie-faced and conceited can you be! she said somewhere inside herself.

Mr Hawthorne would, in his attentive and serious way, reply with the word 'commendable' twice. He would say of both little girls that their behaviour was highly commendable, highly commendable.

Muriel, dressing in a great hurry, her hair still wet, called out to Henry that she was going out to post a letter. She would be back soon, she said, he was not to worry about her, and would he save her some potatoes and to remember that she liked them cold, so no need to heat them.

As she was leaving the house, she paused in the hall. Henry was on the landing, between the two bedrooms, reading aloud from Wordsworth. He was reading from

'The Prelude'. The poem was a favourite choice. Henry's readings soothed her as they soothed the children. He was reading the part where Wordsworth, the boy, steals the shepherd's boat. He unties the boat and takes it out without permission, and rows across the peaceful deep water.

And as I rose upon the stroke, my Boat
went heaving through the water like a swan . . .
The moon was up, the lake was shining clear
Among the hoary mountains; from the shore
I pushed and struck the oars and struck again
In cadenz, and my little Boat mov'd on
Even like a man who walks with stately step,
Though bent on speed. It was an act of stealth
and troubled pleasure; not without the voice
of mountain-echoes did my boat move on,
leaving behind her still on either side
small circles glittering idly in the moon,
until they melted all into one track
of sparkling light . . .

Muriel remembered the description of the way in which the landscape, the mountain crags, dark and sinister, were moving closer as if leaning on him, in pursuit, knowing he had stolen the boat; the mountain was putting strength into the personal feeling of guilt and the image remained in her mind to remind her that Wordsworth, then a mere child, took the little boat back and tied it up safely.

The words of the poem, reaching her as she paused in the hall, almost prevented her from going out on her terrible errand. She surprised herself, calling to Henry that she was going to post a letter when she had no letter. She seemed to be out of breath and she was not even outside the house. She stood for a few minutes in the narrow hall, feeling her clumsy pockets, making sure she had everything she needed. Out in the street she stood near the gate as if undecided.

She arrived at the footbridge without noticing the short walk. It was a dark evening but the clouds, parting, allowed the moonlight to sparkle on raindrops loitering in the packed hedges. A sweet fragrance drifted from the grassy fields. It was a pretty place, not at all the sort of corner for a violent scene. The stormwater drain had its own music as the water rippled and flowed in a little waterfall, beyond the bridge, on its way across the three fields.

Muriel hardly noticed the setting, so concerned was she with her forthcoming deed. She hoped she could carry out her intention. Her loaded pockets were clumsy; her head ached and she could not remember the person's name. The person she had come to see was almost impossible to think about. He knew far too much about her, that was the thought she must keep uppermost. In his disturbed innocence the person might chat to Henry or to other people for that matter, even to Mrs Tonks and Miss Dolly T. She shivered at this extra thought. Such a strange and difficult day this had been and now another thing to deal with. She must hurry, she told herself. Posting a letter could not last all night.

'Victor!' she called his name softly. She had to stand in the water, bending down to look under the bridge. The cold water covered her shoes. She had her little flashlight with her. She pointed the weak yellow light in all directions, all round the timbers of the underside of the bridge. Up and down and round the little beam of light shook and paused, turned back and then up, hovering immediately above her. And then there was a quick little ineffectual flash coming down towards the water. Dark water with the light, her light, playing and dancing over it. The idea of dark water frightened Muriel; you could have no idea what lurked in the mud or in the banks or in the fields.

Once more the weak light explored the timbers of the footbridge. And then, suddenly, she saw him.

Crouched and twisted, knees to chin, his frightened eyes were caught and held in the unsteady beam.

'Victor,' Muriel tried to speak. 'Victor.' She said his name again. She began to rush at him with words, telling him that her pockets were full of things for him. She told him that she knew he loved chocolate and sweets and she had managed to get some for him. He liked money too, she knew this, she told him, and she said she had money for him too. He would, she said, like a bit of money of his own? Everyone, she told him, had some money of their own. She rushed the words at him. She thought it must sound like a gun going off at him, her speaking so quickly and not giving him a chance to see who she was and everything. She had a bit of real money for him; she repeated, word for word, all that she had said. She paused, letting the flashlight shine over his smooth-skinned childish face. He moved quickly, suddenly clumsy in the unexpected light, knocking his head, forehead and cheekbone on the rough timber. The unexpectedly fine skin was immediately bruised, and the grazing on his face began to bleed slowly but steadily, enough to frighten Muriel and, she supposed, Victor. Victor was already frightened at being visited in the dark and in his carefully made hiding place.

145

ELIZABETH JOLLEY

Muriel began then to tell Victor in plain words to take the money and the chocolate and to go back to his foster home. She heard herself threatening Victor that, if he did not go, she would tell the police where he was and they would come and beat him and lock him up. She surprised herself speaking in a grim voice using plain threatening language. She saw the remains of an old army coat clutched in his arms in an attempt to prevent it from falling in the water. He had tied his boots by the laces and had hung them on the underside of one of the supports of the bridge.

She knew that it would be impossible to kill Victor making it look as if he had had an accident of some sort. She would go on frightening him, she told herself, so that he would disappear from their lives completely. Against her will, she thought of the poem again. Wordsworth, as a boy, would be returning the boat and tying her up in the shepherd's hiding place. The feelings of guilt being in evidence from the surrounding mountain crags as they seemed to penetrate *the accusation of the crime . . . the landscape putting strength into personal feeling.*

Victor was so quiet, she thought he must have fainted or gone back to sleep. She called him in a soft voice.

'What is it?' he replied in the abrupt way in which a speech difficulty is dealt with by the person who has it. She promised the chocolate and the money once more, disliking her own voice, a purring, false and untruthful voice. He made no response. She flashed the light on his face. He was still bleeding. He was shivering, white-faced and frightened and, she could see, he was crying quietly. She supposed he was frightened because his face was bleeding. And, of course, she had made some dreadful threats.

Once more she threatened him with a forced removal. 'I shall have to tell the Police you are here,' she said, wishing that she had not started the attack which was both stupid and dreadful.

Suddenly Victor gave a cry which seemed to sound across the three fields and to encapsulate the new unfinished housing estate and the common, this last representing, in a sense, an historic piece of land, a gift to the people, possibly from some time in the Middle Ages. His cry was like the cry of a desperate animal caught in a trap. The sound and then the silence that followed were so terrible Muriel wished for Henry to appear with his usual good sense and affectionate wisdom. Victor was still bleeding. He must have cut his head as well as grazing it, Muriel thought. She must have caused him to cut his head, she corrected herself. He was crying silently, his voice breaking hoarse and helpless, at intervals, through his tears. When he spoke she could not understand him. She noticed, for the first time, his small, clean, useless feet. And, again, she saw his pure clean skin. Just, she thought, as it must have been when he was born. For a moment she thought of his mother, the unknown mother and the newly born son. The picture in her mind was vivid; the small, helpless and deformed baby, wrapped in flannel, being held and rocked in the loving arms of the mother who had just given birth.

This gave Muriel an intense and suddenly deep knowledge of the terrible and wrong thing she had tried to do. How could she, or anyone else, hurt this child, this child-like completely innocent person.

She could only guess the hurtful things which must

have happened to him during his life; hers being one of them. She wanted, all at once, to show Victor her deeply felt shame. She tried to dab, with her handkerchief, the wounds on his forehead and cheekbone. She expected him to pull away from her but he leaned towards her in a perfection of trust. She pushed the money and the chocolate into the pockets of her cardigan. She moved out, backwards, from the cramped space under the bridge.

Suddenly she was afraid that Victor, in his innocent trusting, might realise that she was an enemy, a stupid enemy; and they, the stupid, are the worst sort. She thought he might even attack her. She climbed up the steep bank and he followed her on to the bridge. Holding her handkerchief to his wound, he crouched leaning towards her. He looked as if, in one leap, he would knock her to the ground.

Muriel was weak and frightened, and even more, she was ashamed. Victor did not threaten or look for ways of revenge. He crept towards her, with the usual effort, as near as possible. He held the handkerchief out to her to show her the blood. He stared at the blood and wiped his head again. The blood was slow and showed no signs of stopping. The timbers of the bridge were rough.

Seen in the moonlight they probably seemed almost ordinary to Henry when he came whistling the 'cook-house door, boys' to find Muriel. Muriel, he said, must have walked either to London or to Manchester to post her letter. And now here she was, shamelessly flirting with Victor.

Henry, crouching, pretended to punch Victor. There on the little bridge they charged and wrestled and, leaping and falling, they ducked, avoiding as much as possible any real blows. Victor scooting on 'all fours' almost bowled Henry, as he said, into next week.

Breathless, they paused and Henry said to Victor to come to the kitchen to have his wounds properly dressed. With one arm round Muriel, Henry, quickly with his other hand, pulled the rags of the army coat up round Victor's shoulders. Without realising the irony (as Muriel, in other circumstances, would have liked to point out),

Henry, in cheerful nonsense, said he was always clearing up after his wife. The kitchen fire was still burning, he explained. Did Victor like cocoa or warm milk? Henry wanted to know, there was a choice, he said. And, he said, they would wait while Victor put on his boots.

Muriel, pinning up the blackout curtains, rehearsed some questions she had for Miss Morton (in King's English):

'Oh, Miss Morton, just by the way if you'll pardon the cheek. It's not supposed to be a cheek but, excuse me for asking . . . has, ahem . . . coff . . . coff . . . has Mr Hawthorne, by any chance, has Mr Hawthorne any sort of private embarrassing illness like, um, like a rash on his thighs? Or does he suffer from boils and swollen glands? If so, which parts of the body are affected and which glands? I feel awful asking you a thing like this. I do hope you don't mind my asking but you are the only person who will know things like this . . .'

Henry, during the night, explained that going to London to the opera was not on the same level as deserting your husband and children. He said he was glad she was awake, she had been muttering things in her sleep. He supposed it was the Troll under the Bridge. Or was it a Gnome in the Garden? Nothing serious, he said, her head must be stuffed with nonsense which was escaping. He supposed she was overtired. They were very late to bed after making Victor comfortable on the couch in front of the living-room fireplace. Henry banked up the fire with coal dust and put the fire guard in position. There would be a nice fire in the morning, he told Victor. He promised Victor that he would see that he, Victor, would move to a better foster mother.

Meanwhile Muriel tried to think of the rubbish she had spoken in her disturbed sleep. She was ashamed of her thoughts about Mr Hawthorne having a private illness. Such a silly phrase. She was stupid, she told Henry. She wanted to tell him that she had been very cruel to Victor. She couldn't think of the right words. Henry said she should sleep instead and he would hold her close all night. He was like an electric wire, he said, a flick of the switch and he would be ready. Muriel, aware of her lack of response, after the nightmare on the bridge, said she supposed she was nervous about her journey. Her voice, she thought, had never before sounded so little and silly and self-conscious. She felt ashamed of the conversations which filled her thoughts while Henry was talking seriously about lack of trust and that one person, in a relationship, leaning out towards someone else, could break up a marriage. He told her she was right to worry about certain diseases between men and women. It was well known that disease spread rapidly during a war and this war was no exception. He would, he told her, talk her to sleep, if she would listen. By allowing desire in other directions, the experience (being so rewarding), would be needed often and the two married people could fall apart quickly, he told her. The overpowering wish to explore every aspect of passion and the accompanying awe becomes a need for a repeatedly familiar possession of this other person's body together with the intimate emotional feelings and thoughts. This completeness, this consummation being more satisfying than any other human experience cannot be denied and, as an act of chivalry, the lover is not able to refuse the unspoken, but clearly shown, powerful request.

A person, Henry, like a bee humming, kept on his sleep talk. A person is not unfaithful in other ways except by being untrustworthy, that is by allowing desire for and from another person to persist.

'There was,' he growled, 'there was the difficulty for someone who lives alone, someone who does not have anyone to come home to, in love. Some people live without love and without loving. Some people never have the restoration of the emotional and the spiritual which can be given in both directions in human touch and feeling. And for those who do have the experience, it is not enough to have it simply once. It requires renewal.'

All this was hardly a lullaby, it was a sharp but gently delivered lesson from Henry. Muriel, far from sleeping, had to accept the well-known words in the bitterness of deceit.

While he spoke, his arms were supporting her and holding her. She was accustomed to his strong body and especially his arms with their promise of desire satisfied. Muriel, guilty in her thoughts, was afraid he would know that she was not responding. She told him she was nervous about going away. She knew her voice was the silliest artificial voice. Then, in an even sillier voice, she suggested that they should invite Victor to come and stay with them. Remembering all over again her cruelty, she told Henry that she must 'make it up' to Victor. Henry rolled over, kissing her on her neck. There was no possibility of having Victor to stay, he said. Victor would be shy, he said. 'The house is too small and that is my opinion for what it's worth.'

'Muriel!' Her mother sighing and breathing her name, 'Muriel,' so close to her shoulder when she was putting on her long coat in the hall, 'Muriel,' every moment this disturbing whisper of her name and the sensation of the presence. Muriel, glancing first over the left shoulder and then the right one, said to herself, 'Don't be silly, no one is here,' her voice strained and not like her real voice at all. She hoped she was not ill.

Her mother's too well-remembered voice came back to her with an astonishing clarity when Muriel was on the London train at last. It was as if her mother was about to sit in the empty seat beside her. The train was full, passengers like herself and soldiers, fresh-faced, very young men in new uniforms and boots.

Her mother's voice, still sighing, said she would forever keep her voice low because of the long-eared grandchildren leaning (without manners), *leaning* over the bannister-rail on the landing at the top of the stairs. 'They, the children,' she whispered, 'they listen all the time to everything . . . Muriel!' Her mother, as if still nearby, seemed to be breathing her name all the time and especially when she, Muriel, was putting on her coat.

On the train safely to London. The empty seat remained empty as if for Victor. There would be no reproachings. That was Victor all over. Muriel tried not to think about him. She did not want to remember. She wished she had not been so stupid and cruel. She was unable to stop thinking about him, his name, his twisted innocent face, his purity, his translucence as he tried to see her through the small beam of light from her little flashlight. But mostly it was the cry in his voice which refused to fade.

Victor, aided by Henry, gave his little speech of thanks for the warm couch. There was no suggestion of subdued anger towards her. He gave her a shy sort of smile as if saying that they, together, could keep their little secret. A sure way for Muriel to dread the suggestion of hiding her cruel and pointless attack until such time Victor might want to make use of it.

When Muriel hastily, within minutes of setting off for the railway station, confessed to Henry her tremendous uneasiness over her awful behaviour towards Victor, he simply said to her to forget the whole thing.

Victor, Henry said, hadn't an ounce of revenge in

him. So Muriel must stop thinking about it. Unprofitable thoughts, as in this case, were a waste of energy.

All the same she knew that Henry did not ignore her guilt. He might even be thoroughly shocked but choosing, at this particular time, before her journey, to make light of the whole thing.

She was on her way to Mr Hawthorne. Mr Hawthorne would be fond and calm and kind. He would be quick with wisdom. He had endless strength and the needed solutions, as he had in tennis. The pleasure of watching him during a serious game would never be forgotten. She could bring the memory close. Mr Hawthorne, master of a calculating watchfulness and movement, in complete command as he ran, leaping, almost to the net to smash the ball back and beyond the reach of his opponent but all within the boundaries of the game. She saw his power contained in the white flannels always in movement in the position, the best position for anticipation, for knowing his next movement of forceful strength, judgement and restraint as the score mounted in his favour.

In the train Muriel gave herself up to the soothing and reliable rhythm, knowing that she was travelling in the right direction. There was no Victor. She was leaving Victor. She would like some kind person to take care of Victor. Victor would be cleared away by an authority trained to know what was best for him, Victor. She hoped someone kind and good . . .

In the short quick discussion Henry said again that it was not possible for Victor to stay with them, much as he wanted to help Victor. It would be foolish, he said, even criminal to try to do something so much in the face of being entirely inadequate.

Muriel had forgotten the pleasure of the longer railway journey. Her work needed ten to fifteen minutes by train with a walk at either end. The bus took longer, going round some suburban streets, stopping more frequently. Walk at both ends much the same as the railway. Buses and trains were overcrowded before the war and were more so during the war. Overcrowded and often late.

Railway waiting rooms more dismal and the expected warmth from the fireplace missing. Henry rode his bicycle most of the time, he liked the independence.

Muriel thought for a moment that, because of their work, Henry had not had a holiday for years. And, of course, neither had she. She felt caressed in the soothing, reliable rhythm of the train. She was leaving the city where she lived (on the edges only), Henry trying to believe that they, in the unfinished new housing estate, were practically in the country. He imagined, Muriel said, villages, trees, old churches and cemeteries, and a wonderful relaxed atmosphere in both the weather and the people, as if the English Midlands, the Black Country, had some hitherto unknown beautiful parkland, the common and a few left-over farms and hawthorn hedges and at least three known fields, or meadows as some preferred to call them. Muriel was travelling to the city of London. She was in awe of this place and was making the journey with courage and hope.

She was leaving the Midlands, the churches, the schools, the factories, the coal mines, the brickworks, the chimneys, the bone and glue shops, the suburb and housing estates . . . She let the rest of the list drop away from her thoughts. She felt completely rested. She stared at other people at times when they dozed or looked with vacant eyes towards the windows. Sliding alongside were different but expected landscapes, the slopes and the valleys, the woods and the spinneys, those dark spindles of trees grown especially for the flushing out of the game birds for the ardent and hopeful huntsmen. Upper class, of course.

Railway stations, on the way, remained anonymous in coats of thick white and dark brown paint.

Sometimes the train rattled over a level crossing where patient people in cars waited and children, walking with their mothers, paused to wave to the train.

Sometimes there was a stream, its winding course marked by ancient willow trees. And, in the meadows, cattle, grazing, lifted their heads in the direction of the train for a few moments before returning to their industrious feeding.

I'm on my way to Him, to Mr Hawthorne, Muriel

gave herself courage as the light was changing to an autumnal dusk, bringing a reminder of the change to sorrow, homelessness, poverty and loneliness. She shuddered. What if Mr Hawthorne had forgotten she was coming. Or worse; what if Mr Hawthorne had an intrusive housekeeper and, or, an intrusive lover. She imagined the girl, tall and blonde and sophisticated, perched on the arm of Mr Hawthorne's chair while Miss Morton stood, humble and patient, with a tray laden with tea cups and saucers, waiting for the girl to remember her manners and, at the same time, to Mind Her State. A favourite sentiment of down-to-earth, speaking-their-minds housekeepers, especially when they are protecting their own particular Mr Gentleman. And, of course, the same phrase could prevent a lady from forgetting that she was a lady and, in the eyes of Miss Morton, that might be her only qualification, and worth keeping.

Muriel, with relief, remembered that she was not responsible for or to Miss Morton. She was merely jealous of her. In every detail of position and dress and usefulness, this unknown woman had qualities which

Muriel felt unable to possess. The jealousy was painful, the more so because they had never met.

Muriel returned in her thoughts to wishing for Mr H. He would be strong and careful and intent on an excellent performance. His body and his emotional thoughts were all in place for her. She knew that he had never been attracted to anyone before. He confessed, earlier, that Henry and Muriel together were so complete, he both envied and enjoyed their delicate sense of harmony. They, Muriel and Mr Hawthorne, had talked about this on the bridge.

'You're so sweet,' Muriel remembered the phrase especially because Mr H. had been so pleased at it being said to him when he had not expected it.

Muriel, if she had known Miss Morton at all, felt that she might have been able to ask for an opinion on Mr Hawthorne's health. Surprised and rather ashamed of herself and her thoughts, she glanced quickly at the other passengers. They were all rocking, swaying slightly, giving themselves up to the rhythm of the train. She wondered if any of these people had asked about the health of a possible lover as the 'Health during the War' notices suggested. She wondered if any of these silent travellers had lovers as she had Mr Hawthorne. They did not look as if they would ask any person about private health details. Fortunately she had not asked anything about Mr Gentleman Hawthorne, she smiled at the addition, in thought, to his name. She could not imagine considering curiosity about Mr Hawthorne's private health. She wondered if she was suffering from an obsession.

Muriel thought next of Henry. Miss Tonks was to mind the children till their father came from school. She did not want to think of Henry but, in her mind, she saw them all in the kitchen peeling potatoes to boil them in salty water and then to have real butter (she had saved some), on the hot potatoes. Miss Tonks had insisted on bringing a Queen's Pudding over for the second course. The Queen of Puddings to be announced!

She tried once more not to go over the little scene again. She felt homesick and frightened and told herself

that she could take a train straight back if she did want
to go home. There was so much about the journey which
she could not know in advance. She could only imagine
at present. She thought about their love, which she tried
to think of without anxious scenes being made in her
nervous thinking. She told herself that Mr H. *wanted to
hear and see* Fidelio *with her*.

Mr H., Henry said, before she left, was strong and
solid, he was a large man, large in body and in kindness.
And she was pretty and clever and reliable. And she
could deliver a lecture and even a second and a third and
know what she was talking about.

Henry, himself, was small and muscular. A beautiful
body, Muriel told him. He was more like a coal miner
than a teacher. Henry explained it was as if his father had
kept him gnarled and small and tough in readiness for the
work in which he would need to be able to creep in the
narrow places between the rock face and the coal seam.
A father and a mother, he said, could be quite mistaken
in their idea of the particular work or study the child
chooses to take up, or takes up without a choice.

'You're sweet,' Muriel told Mr Hawthorne more than once. 'You're so innocent and sweet.' His kiss, in reply then, was loving and slow. He told her that he meant every second of his kiss. He told her she was exquisite in so many ways and if he could be with her just for one whole night he would spend the time thanking her and showing her how much he loved her.

The train was all at once cautiously within the outskirts of London. The city was in darkness. Some street lamps were on but dim as if strangled by the oncoming dusk and the remnants of fog. Muriel let the other passengers remove their luggage and themselves first. Suddenly alone and self-conscious in the deserted railway compartment, she wished for Henry, really needing his quick knowledge of what to do next. She felt shy and awkward and, stupidly, she wished for her mother to appear, taking charge with flamboyant and elegant (her own word) charm of the next part of the journey. A fellow passenger, wordlessly, put Muriel's small case on the seat. She grabbed the handle of her case and, lacking the better manners of travelling, she did not thank the young man who had carefully lifted it down from the overhead rack. She stepped down on to the platform.

People were still hurrying towards the exit. She felt that she was the only person who did not know where to go next. She tried not to be frightened in the crowds, but rather to look happily about her, to find Mr Hawthorne. No familiar figure or face came from the other end of the busy platform. She tried to remind herself of her own confidence. She had the ability to enter the classroom and to deliver a lecture and to teach someone something they had never known before. She would think about teaching. She noticed quite quickly that many travellers had a gas mask in a special case slung on one shoulder. She should have brought hers.

'What a pity you did not manage to travel together.' Mr Hawthorne, the welcome material of his coat and his kind, quiet face emerged from the darkness of the station.

ELIZABETH JOLLEY

And then Muriel saw Miss Morton at Mr Hawthorne's side. Miss Morton's rich laughter made light of the fact that she had tried to find Mrs Bell.

'We must have been in different parts of this rather long train,' she said. Muriel thought how well Miss Morton's laugh suited her and matched her clothes. She wore a tailored costume, a jacket and skirt complete with a little round hat decorated with scraps of veiling material. Muriel, seeing this example of good taste, wished that she could climb the elusive social ladder with an intimate appreciation from one woman to the other. She wished to be equal with good quality cloth and the cheeky little hat, all of which Miss Morton's graceful deportment carried so well in spite of Miss Morton's stout, comfortable appearance. Miss Morton was a large woman, well bred (as Muriel had expected), and graceful in spite of her size. She certainly presented an appearance. For Muriel she presented an anxiety. An extra person.

In the moments of pause and gaze and the shy smiles of greeting, Mr Hawthorne really had eyes only for

Muriel. He moved towards her, looking into her eyes as if from a great height. In silence, in a small intimate movement towards her, he lifted with one finger a strand of her fair, soft hair, placing it gently behind her left ear. This action, while being restrained and gentle with well-bred tenderness and elegance, in the presence of Miss Morton, was a gentle statement of loving and possession. This was extended as his fingertips, lightly moving, caressed the smooth curve of Muriel's softly rounded cheek while he withdrew his audacious finger. Mr Hawthorne, keeping her within his gaze, moved back a little but his intention, his direction and his smile remained and maintained the silent moment of worship. His eyes, Muriel felt, would keep her sweetly close. In silence they all moved towards the way out.

The modest little scene, in perfect taste, ended. Mr Hawthorne called the one remaining porter (the war, he explained, had absorbed all the others). The taxi came and Miss Morton and her luggage were stowed in the car. Muriel realised that Miss Morton was going to the same hotel. Relaxed after Mr Hawthorne's 'hairdressing',

Muriel was anxious once more. Miss Morton had clearly come to town, to the city, to stay, with so much luggage; and Muriel was afraid that she was *really expected at the same hotel*. She began to make little scenes in her mind, Miss Morton having noisy cold baths or long hot baths so that the hotel bathroom was never free. Miss Morton suggesting cheerfully that in the morning they could wait for each other and go down to hotel brekkers together. Herself and Miss Morton like two upper-school, upper-class schoolgirls out from their boarding school and in a hotel instead of staying with an ancient relative or a reliable previous teacher from their school . . .

Muriel once again was thinking she must go home. She felt alone once more when Mr Hawthorne, gossiping with Miss Morton, leaned into the cab.

'Goodbye, Morton, my regards to Sarah.'

Muriel was still thinking that she should go home. City life (her own cliché) made her feel excluded. Mr Hawthorne seemed to be, forever, leaning into Miss Morton's cab.

'Goodbye, Morton, Old Thing,' he said, 'do give my

Best to Sarah.' Muriel listened to him repeating himself the way in which people do when they are trying not to look impatient, but are really wanting the traveller to be off on the way. Muriel, feeling suddenly fond, was glad Mr Hawthorne was disposing of Miss Morton. And then stupidly, as she told herself, she was anticipating more worry. She realised how alone a person was in a large city where even the pavements were completely unconcerned. She was afraid that there would not be enough tickets for *Fidelio*. She felt she would not mind missing the opera. It was, after all, a troubled and a troubling piece. Many people, including the experienced critics, at the time, did not think well of it. Swiftly she allowed another thought to blossom. It was certainly a well-known truth that people who were fond of each other, in love with each other, very often could not explain or deal with a situation which then became unwieldy between them. She thought she must remember to remind Henry that this was a great truth which had travelled alongside literature and society since the time of Euripides (and others). For example, Electra refuses to believe that certain footprints could be her brother's. She denies the suggestion because it is their destiny to kill their own mother when the two of them, together, Orestes and Electra, meet their own mother, all being forced to recognise each other. Similarly, Jason is never able to explain to Medea that he is leaving her, and her sons, in order to marry the princess, daughter of King Creon, who wants a son-in-law because he has no sons of his own. Jason has no courage and no truthful way in which to offer a good reason for his actions, and Orestes and Electra (the brother and sister) are dealing with Blood Feud, which has only one remedy.

He, Henry the nimble, the quick, red-brown fox would understand at once. He would enjoy, yet again, the knowledge being assimilated. If only she could talk to him about Mr Hawthorne, he would be sure to understand. But there the thought was forced to end. Another group of fresh-faced, innocent young men in new uniforms were marching towards the entrance to the railway station. Muriel, staring at them, wondered if there would be trouble with *Fidelio*. Some English people would protest about the expensive production of a German opera during a war. She thought how she might give her ticket away (if there was one to give away), and then make for the railway station and simply wait in an obscure and bleak waiting room till a train to the Midlands was announced.

More troublesome was the company of Miss Morton and now someone called Sarah. Muriel's jealousy thrived, bringing the usual pain and guilt.

'Mr Hawthorne's a good man.' Henry would not easily change his opinion.

'Morton's a good fellow,' Mr Hawthorne said. He explained that Morton's younger sister was promised a trip to Paris but the war had prevented this and so they were off to the Lake District for a few days. Sarah was his nursemaid, Mr Hawthorne said, a long time ago. A long long time ago. 'I loved her very much,' he said.

Mr Hawthorne caught Muriel's arm and drew her close to him. He had her little overnight bag in his other hand but this did not prevent him from holding her with a gentle fondness. Muriel felt ashamed, she could not say to Mr Hawthorne that she was frightened and anxious and shamefully jealous. Jealousy, she knew, could spoil everything, especially a kiss. He stopped walking and there in the street he kissed her even though people were passing. His kiss was gentle and tender and she was immediately comforted. It was all a part of reality, Mr Hawthorne's reality, Muriel thought, his impeccable good manners and restrained intimate conversation suggesting that he was really in love with an intense passion, when it was simply the behaviour belonging to his trained, well-mannered attitude and ways of thinking.

Still in Mr Hawthorne's arms, Muriel surprised herself that this would be Henry's way of an examination of human behaviour. To her surprise she suddenly began to cry. She sobbed so much that a passing policeman stopped and asked what the trouble was. Mr Hawthorne immediately, in an even voice, explained that they were both emotional having been separated for a long time.

'That's the war for you,' the officer, hardly pausing on his beat, said. 'Good morning all.'

It did seem that the morning was beginning to show in the sky. Muriel saw an anxious glance as Mr

Hawthorne looked at her as if she was only a little schoolgirl. 'Perhaps we should go at once to your hotel,' he said. 'I'm afraid we must walk. I don't see a taxi.' Muriel nodded. She had noticed the hotel was 'hers' not 'ours'. Mr Hawthorne must, she thought, have seen her quick disappointment. Already her eyes were overflowing with tears. She must not cry, she thought. Mr H. will not know how to handle this whole situation.

Muriel said she would like two picture postcards to send to the little girls. Mr Hawthorne said it was an easy request because the hotel had cards at the reception desk. He went on to say that his demands were not so reticent. He was, he said, impatient for her. He wanted, he said, to be simply with her, more than the opera, he said. No one, he said, can know how much he had missed her and how much he had looked forward to her visit. 'Of course,' he said, giving her a little hug as he quickened his step, 'of course, I couldn't write to you in that sort of way, could I.'

Muriel thought Mr Hawthorne was looking very tired and said so. Yes, she thought, they were both tired.

'I am hoping,' he said, 'to be not too late to bed . . . tonight!' He smiled and she could see his kind face in spite of another rush of tears. 'We're almost there,' he said.

Jealous people always feel guilty for being jealous, she told herself. Miss Morton was obviously a thoroughly good sort, that would be how Mr Hawthorne thought of her. Muriel was deeply ashamed of the vulgarity of her jealousy. She continued to frighten herself with thoughts which Henry would dismiss as unprofitable. Perhaps Miss Morton was more than a good housekeeper for Mr Hawthorne. There seemed to be an intimacy of goodwill between them. She told herself that it was natural, having lived in the same house together for a very long time, for them to have family jokes and understandings between them.

It might even be that they do share the same bedroom. Muriel tried to imagine the substantial nightdress, winceyette or some such material in an outrageously ugly garment, to put out of mind the very delicate pretty gown, black and pink, mostly made of lace.

This last garment, hardly existing but refusing to give way, caused Muriel to feel that she really did want to get safely back to Henry and a simple life.

But what would Henry think and do and say? He would only believe in the best and the good over Mr Hawthorne. As for herself, he, Henry, would not see her as she so well saw herself. He might call her a tart but that was for fun only and was changed at once to jam or custard. It was impossible for her to offer and for him to accept the real reason for her early homecoming.

Mr Hawthorne was just saying that the hotel was on the next corner. She could see how close it was, when all at once the air-raid sirens started up and the policeman, complete with his tin hat and gas mask, was coming towards them, sending people into an air-raid shelter very close to where they were walking. Mr Hawthorne explained that they were just a few steps from their hotel. The officer said he was simply carrying out his duties. The siren, swooping, insisted.

'Into the shelter if you please, sir. Shelter, madam.'

The shelter was dark and already a number of people were there. Muriel, unable to help herself, began to cry again. She felt ashamed, at the same time, she told him, because a woman had a toddler with her and a very young baby, both children were very pale and the mother herself looked worn out. She, in her silly way, began again to be anxious and guilty. Mr Hawthorne sat down on a wooden bench just inside the entrance, but down some horrible (Muriel said), dirty steps. Mr Hawthorne said to Muriel to sit on his lap and sleep a little if she could. He seemed to be surprisingly unselfconscious and she thought she would try to emulate him. Everything was different from expectations.

A few babies and children cried. A young woman had to be taken away in an ambulance. A woman sitting nearby explained that the sirens going off had brought it on. 'The childbirth,' she said. 'Happens all the time,' she said, taking out her knitting.

For Muriel, the accents, being so different from other parts of England, gave the scene an air of unreality which, in itself, was restful and brave.

The people in the air-raid shelter seemed to know each other. Some had packed sandwiches and cake and some poured coffee from shabby old flasks. One man had a mouth organ. Smiling, he announced his music. Some people talked to each other and some slept. It was clear that they were used to coming into the shelter.

Muriel could not sleep. She still felt guilty, almost as if guilt was a pleasure. She could not understand her lack of courage and her unhappiness during the day. And here was Mr Hawthorne, peaceful, and full of love for her. She rested her head against his shoulder.

At times the throbbing engines of the aeroplanes could be heard, and those who knew declared which were English planes and which were the enemy. Frightening sounds, as of explosions, came closer and seemed to be overhead, one after the other. Someone screamed and others wept and still others were silent. Mr Hawthorne made Muriel lie across his lap. He said they were safe and she must rest as comfortably as she could. An old man recited the Lord's Prayer and from all parts of the shelter there came a series of responses, including the mouth organ.

Prayers were easy, Muriel reflected, when there was danger. She admitted to herself that, in the way that she lived, her prayers, if remembered, were trivial in comparison with this prayer. Her lips were close to Mr Hawthorne's ear and the side of his face. His face was warm to her face. Feeling happy and grateful, she gave his ear and his cheek some little soft kisses and he tightened his arms round her, responding secretly, she supposed, to her secret approach.

It would be easy, Muriel thought, to experience good manners in the company of a refined, handsome, educated gentleman and then to make the mistake of confusing good habits and manners with imaginative thoughts that he was deeply in love . . . She wanted to say something of this to Mr Hawthorne. She supposed she had always wanted some kind of declaration and understanding from him. Something which would give her rights, as it were, in the presence of Miss Morton or within Miss Morton's rights of possession. Possibly she would find that she had no rights. She wanted to tell Mr Hawthorne 'thank you' for looking after her in the air-raid shelter. He had explained to her that he was nursing her on the impatience of his lap and, he wanted to know, was this uncomfortable for her? He had wanted her to feel his presence in this way. Because of this, when he had been so outspoken, she wanted to tell him she was aching to have him nearer and not covered up.

There was no chance for the opera now and she would not need to pretend to be sad about this.

The All Clear sirens roused her from an unrestful sleep. People were leaving the shelter, subdued and stiff and thankful. Children cried. The steady sound of the All Clear sirens began to fade.

Outside the shelter the sky was streaked with the promise of the tender sunrise. And they saw at once a changed scene. The whole area was roped off and the boundaries were marked by small lights in tin containers.

Where the street had been, there was a ragged crater, a deep hole in the road. Black ash and evil-smelling smoke hovered. People were coughing as they tried to hurry away. Across the street an apartment house had been stripped all down one side. Searchlights, in a slow-moving fan across the sky, revealed the pink and blue plaster work of the walls in a series of bathrooms, one above the other – but in danger of collapsing, as one man said, as he walked alongside the rope round to the far side of the crater. Mr Hawthorne said that they, himself and Muriel, should walk that way. The bathroom fittings unattached, Mr Hawthorne said, looked like ugly decorations for an unwanted ceremony.

The young mother changed her baby's nappy at the edge of the crater. Muriel watching, as the people moved forward slowly, saw the baby boy's tiny penis exposed, for a few moments, but long enough to remind her how delicate life was and how quickly Victor had snatched the baby guinea pigs from the soaked baby clothes which would have drowned them at once. The little girls had described the scene so well, each one taking an imagined memory and relating it, unharmed, at home. She felt she had seen it all.

Mr Hawthorne told Muriel, as they walked up the hill to the hotel, that he felt that the air-raid warning had been like a kind of permission, as if telling them to take each other in their feelings of love and respect since there was a chance that either or both of them might be destroyed before the next morning, a sort of *laissez-aller, laissez-faire, an abstaining-from-interference attitude*. He thought that even if the whole attitude was simply a kind of cliché or simply wishful thinking, Henry might be willing and prepared to accept and continue to cherish all that belonged to him, completely, to cherish. He did intend, he said, to see Henry alone, not to apologise exactly but simply to speak of his own weakness and the sweet gentle beauty which rightfully belonged to Henry. Henry, he was certain, would not insist on a duel . . .

Muriel was weeping silently and Mr Hawthorne wiped away her tears before the doors of the hotel were opened.

Muriel was surprised to see tears on Mr Hawthorne's face. These tears made her understand the need for her tears to be for someone else, not the usual ones just for herself. She supposed, surprising herself with an unaccustomed honesty, she supposed she cried mostly out of self-pity.

Because of wartime restrictions Muriel had expected the hotel to be rather overcrowded and dreary. It was, she said, especially nice to meet someone who seemed to be so friendly. The night porter, who opened the doors for them, was known to Mr Hawthorne. The porter made air-raid-relief jokes and reminded Mr Hawthorne of his (the porter's) position as night porter at the door of Mr Hawthorne's club just across the street. He was into two jobs, he explained, the war having taken plenty of men. He had seen the bank notes folded in the palm of Mr Hawthorne's hand, and yes he would send up a pot of tea and sandwiches to the rooms. And, yes, there was plenty of water for hot baths. Breakfast up till ten-thirty in the morning, and, yes, he would put a telegram through right away if his Lordship would give him the details. He thought, he said, that the lady needs a cognac and, of course, the usual for his Lordship, a single malt, hard to come by these days, but then the reputation of the Club had to be revered. He had the very special one. He winked and was gone.

The tea (stewed) was delivered, also warm towels. Mr Hawthorne held out his arms to Muriel, who rested in his embrace while he told her that he loved her forever and would never love anyone else. He said that he could never have first place in her heart because of her belonging to Henry. 'I do love you so much,' he repeated the important little words; 'all the same, I do love you so very much.'

Muriel leaned on to his chest, crying, the tears in her eyelashes like shining jewels. 'I can't live without you,' she sobbed. 'I want to be with you, *please*.' Mr Hawthorne held her close and spoke in a very gentle way, telling her they could either be together for the rest of the night or they could have a room each. He showed her the little dressing room with its narrow bed and the gentleman's wardrobe with its stale smell of cigars. He told her to choose.

Mr Hawthorne's dressing gown was made of silk. It was smooth, caressing her nakedness. A gentleman's dressing gown, she thought. She was full of worrying thoughts, she explained to Mr Hawthorne. She kept crying even though she was so pleased to be with him. It was Henry, she explained. He had come to the station with her. He looked thin and pale and he had walked alongside the train as it crept away from the platform. He had walked and started running for as long as he could and, then, as he waved, the train followed the well-known curve away from the empty platform and then was off on the journey south to London. And then it was impossible to see him any more.

'In Henry's own language,' Mr Hawthorne said, 'he would say you were being silly.' Muriel had to agree. He reminded her that Henry would receive the telegram, first thing, and know that she was safe.

When the tea (stewed in the porter's lodge) had been poured and attention drawn to the warm towels in the bathroom cupboard, Mr Hawthorne asked if he could help Muriel into the deep bath. She might need help getting out of it, he said. He liked, he said, the good old-fashioned furniture. He stood beside her to help her take off the dressing gown. Drawing her nakedness towards himself, he kissed her and, while still standing, he lifted her, as if over the tennis net and into his own court.

'Be quick in the bath,' Muriel said.

'I'll be quick,' he said, 'wait for me.' In the little pause it was like a special moment, so special it was like a gift being given to them both. Simultaneously. A solemn moment. 'I can't give you all the love you ought to have,' Mr Hawthorne said, 'because you belong to someone else.' He tucked the bedclothes round her. 'But I am giving it. Remember, *Today you are with me.*

'*Heute, heute, bist du mit mir,*' he sang softly.

'*Heute, heute, bist du mit mir.*' The soft sound of his restrained singing in the bathroom reached her. Smiling to herself, she listened to Bach's timeless musical permission and waited for the Divine rescue.

He came, the Lover, and with capable hands he explored her body. With his lips he kissed her all over. 'This is worship,' she heard him breathe the words on her smoothness. 'Worship is not enough,' he said, 'it's a serious game with serious rules.' He touched her in all the places and she moved as if at his request. This tender examination, she felt, guided him to know her body, her mind and her emotional need. Feeling the reaction in herself, she moved gently beneath him as she guided him to his advantage. She knew from the intensity in his movements and his expression, the slight and cautious hesitation, the pause as if he was waiting for her, holding back the pleasure of responsibility, of an exquisite sensation of passion and sensuality, culminating in an even greater desire for the one person to be simultaneously drawn towards, and held, during the timeless moment of each one for the other, giving way, experiencing, each one for the other, the Divine Responsibility for the sensations which held them both, in these moments, as one. Muriel felt her satisfying reactions were directly from Mr Hawthorne and she gave herself up completely to his rhythm of movement and breathing.

As if soothed, Mr Hawthorne rested his head beside hers, on her pillow. She knew he needed to sleep. In her moments of deep warmth and satisfaction, Muriel, without meaning to, thought about Henry. Everything, she told herself, would be so much easier if he was a thoroughly bad and mean man.

*A*ccustomed to telling Henry every detail in small daily adventures, discoveries in books, discoveries about people and things seen in the marketplace or the rough unfinished roads and avenues of the Estate, things the children said or did . . . anything really that came in her thoughts. She, from habit, simply started relating the first things in her mind as soon as she heard his key in the front door and his step up into the hall. Her grievances came out all too quickly and had to be repeated at once as Henry, tired from his day at school, tried to shed the many school-time worries before trying to deal with Muriel's repetitive complaints.

Muriel's thoughts, occupied with Mr Hawthorne, prevented her from regaling Henry immediately. She, in any case, could not offer what was uppermost, in her mind, to Henry. She realised that since her return from London, she thought about Mr Hawthorne every few minutes. She re-lived the ways in which he had caressed her, holding her in different positions in the strength of his well-made limbs and body. She thought about his careful movements as his desire for her excited her and she responded to his mounting ardour.

It was like remembering a dance and wishing for the movement and the steps, the particular closeness to the dancing partner, and the particular rhythm of the music all over again. Every few minutes during the day and, at times in the night, she thought about Mr Hawthorne, all the time wishing she was free to be able to be with him. She was unable to stop thinking about his smooth loving hands. She wanted him in every possible detail of loving. She wanted to feel his arms round her. Some weeks had gone by yet her thoughts had not given up. She had no inclination for food or for walks. The children, she said, made her tired. Could Henry come home early and take them in the fields? Or could Henry do their bath and supper?

When Henry came home he went straight upstairs to the dressing table. He was writing a letter to Mr

Hawthorne. He felt he must see Mr Hawthorne as quickly as possible. He had all the dates clearly written down. He supposed Muriel had overlooked this 'aspect of life'. He did not like the cliché but understood that the cliché was often the best way to write something. The cliché is easily understood and quickly understood, he added this fact to the letter in case Mr H. was not accustomed to cliché of the particular sort he was using. He was surprised at his own reactions and even more surprised about Mr H. and his apparent behaviour.

'What did you expect?' Mrs Tonks, who was on the same bus, had patted the seat next to her. Without saying too much, Henry hinted, in as nice a way as possible, the problem, an entirely new problem.

'What did you expect!' Mrs Tonks was blunt. 'You're a man yerself, ain't you. Yo've been made a fool of yerself that's what I can see.' Henry said that he agreed with her.

'A man like him's too kind and perlite to say "no" to a sweet purtie little creature, your wife. Pardon me if I'm too plain in what I'm saying.' She patted Henry on the shoulder and picked up her handbag. 'She was getting off the bus early,' she explained. 'She was just popping into the corner shop for milk,' she said. 'You'll be having extra milk and juice, that'll be nice.' She nodded, approving of Henry in every way. She bent down as the bus was slowing. 'What you've jus' tole me, it shan't go no further than us two,' she said. 'Just let her settle down to it, a bit, that's the best way. And don't you be bothered by other people and what they might be thinking and saying.'

Henry felt relieved and grateful. Mrs Tonks had been so plainly unworried. Of course it was not a problem for her and the Tonkette. All the same, he had to admit, he felt comforted by the few words. The reaction to his confidential whisper was soothing.

'Are you all right?' Henry took the tumbler from Muriel's cold hand. He saw the bottle on the table. He felt cheated in every possible way. He supposed Muriel imagined she could get rid of the baby by drinking the cheap sherry. She kept wanting more. The consolation was that there would be no more. That was final, Henry decided. He took her in his arms. He told her she must drink water if she was still in the desert.

'Lots of fresh water,' he said, making light of an extra problem. 'I'll finish this,' he said, taking the bottle from her other hand. She had said earlier, he reminded her that neither of them knew anything about wine except that after having some, they were both likely to feel depressed and argumentative. Especially Henry, who was known to be sick if he had too much. She reminded him of this, the accusation all too clearly in her eyes and in the tone of her voice. Because of this unhappiness, Henry felt obliged to come home earlier than he should from school. Muriel understood the seriousness of his absence from his boys at the end of the afternoon and modified her behaviour in the smallest way that she could.

On the second night in London Mr Hawthorne and Muriel left the opera just before the end and had their baths early. They went straight to bed. As Mr Hawthorne said, he was an impatient lover and Leonore's sufferings had gone on rather a long time. 'Just a quick bath,' he said then, picking her up and putting her into the warm water.

It did not matter then or now, in retrospect, as Muriel went over in her thoughts, Mr Hawthorne's desire and his being too quick for her, 'Too much in advance,' were his words, she recalled his dismay. They were still Mrs Bell and Mr Hawthorne, neither of them chose to change this. She recalled frequently his sweet confession and his returning desire, this being as strong as ever and *for her*.

The boredom of the small house on the Estate was worse for Muriel as the days unfolded. She had no wish, no heart, she explained, to make meals. Henry boiled the potatoes and the carrots. He baked them, using the whole oven by putting a sweet rice pudding to cook at the bottom of the oven. He showed the little girls how to do this. He put grated cheese on top of a dish of left-over cabbage. He had the pleasure of pulling a cabbage, planted by himself, for their dinner.

Henry, escaping to the bedroom and the cleared dressing table, read right through his collection of notes in the red exercise book. Several Sundays and the weeks in between had gone by. His idea of a meeting, a confrontation meeting with Mr H., was put together in his mind immediately before the usual Sunday dinner. Muriel's mother, as always, was present. Mr Hawthorne was not present as he had not yet been invited. Henry thought it was a long way to come for one of their Sunday dinners but it was clear there must be some important constructive discussion.

The dates and comments in the notebook were very useful for his diagnosis. Because her symptoms were exactly similar to those experienced when she was, as she called it, in 'the family way' twice before, Henry made a note in the red book. He favoured the word 'pregnant', or 'cyesis' was even better, more professional. The restless nights, the morning sickness ('nausea' was better) and, all at once the tender breasts and the swollen legs, 'oedema' a better word, i.e. swollen legs. The fact that Muriel recalled all these changes in her body, when her two previous babies were expected, made her even more certain that Henry was also the father of this baby, if there really was a baby. It was a fault in Henry that this condition, pushed on to her, must be from him, she was bearing all the same symptoms. Also, she explained, that just before she went to London she had given away the pram and the cot, the whole caboodle of baby clothes, stacks of nappies. It was just like the thing. People said you should never give away anything. She howled with the sheer annoyance of it all . . .

Muriel was annoyed that Henry could do this common thing, the growing of cabbages in the empty garden. And this was made worse by his giving cabbages to other people, strangers, complete strangers, really. What would they be thinking . . . these other people?

Henry was unable to understand her misgivings. He knew how pleased he was with a fresh crisp cabbage. He was impatient to have his garden filled with all vegetables in time. *These days, it was important to have something to cook.* 'Good year for cabbage,' a man, going by, nodded and spoke to Henry, who enjoyed the moment. Later he described the man to Muriel. In a sort of tantrum she declared she would never be able to set foot outside the house because of Henry and his *common* vegetables.

Henry tried to be sympathetic. Muriel was upset rather than ill. She said it was the long journey, and the filthy air-raid shelter. Food made her sickness worse even when the little girls, to please her, made a salad with sweet-pea flowers all round the dish – a suggestion from Mrs Tonks who had these flowers in her garden, already, a whole fence full of them.

Muriel tried not to dislike food and she, at last, acknowledged that she did have a baby inside her. A letter from Mr Hawthorne to Henry seemed to cure her, and she was sensible enough to know that Mr H. could not write, as he would really want to write, to her. His letter was short. He was coming north, he wrote, and would love to see them. He gave a date with sufficient time ahead. Henry was delighted with such kind thoughtfulness. He was still trying to compose a letter to Mr H.

It seemed that Mr H. would soon be with them. He was coming because of his work but his *wish* to come was to see them, the family, as he thought of them all. There seemed, to Muriel, to be a restrained little message especially for her 'between the lines' of neat, restrained legal handwriting. She had a whole set of memories. One, from before her two nights in London, was of a short train journey after class, one night, when Mr Hawthorne insisted on travelling with her even though it meant he would be very late home. The train was full of soldiers, young new recruits, in new uniforms. Mr Hawthorne and Muriel were standing close together, packed close in the crowded corridor of the train. The memory was of Mr H. holding and steadying her body in the sweetest way against himself as the train, gathering speed, swayed and rocked.

Another vivid thought, during family mealtimes, was of lying beside Mr H. while he slept. She wondered if he dreamed of their apotheosis in the triumphant early morning, waking up to sweet wickedness (his phrase). She remembered, suddenly, Leonie, self-appointed college friend and mentor in all things sexual. Leonie, she remembered, explained how the trumpet, in an orchestral work, with small delicate intrusions lightly penetrates the early movements in a symphony, for example, Beethoven's seventh symphony, and finally breaks through in full triumphant sound in the last movement with the orchestra building up to a deeply satisfying completeness of desire with yet other sounds blending; an apotheosis, which both haunts and fulfils all promises.

When questioned, Leonie would shrug her shoulders, saying, 'So? Where do people get their knowledge?'

For Muriel this, at that time, seemed brave, daring and thrilling. In her dream world, she told herself, now, she was experienced, sweetly experienced.

In the packed corridor, in the short railway journey, Muriel had looked up, and in the subdued lighting, she had seen how delicate and sensitive Mr Hawthorne's expression could be. Mischievous and kind and, above all, tender. She would, she told herself often, keep his face in her mind forever. A hundred times a day she told him silently, somewhere inside herself, she told him that she was in love with him.

Accepting a cup of tea from Henry, she told him that she wanted *simply and really, that she wanted to be with Mr Hawthorne or, at least to talk about him*. A sudden screaming from the two little girls, over a doll, ended the almost careless remark about Mr H. as Henry was obliged to end a domestic, but war-like, scene in the bedroom. Meanwhile Muriel drank more tea. Naturally, the war affected families, she sighed over the empty teapot.

Earlier, Muriel teaching the little girls, cut up an apple into halves and then one half into quarters. The remains of the lesson were on the table. It was decided earlier that the mother would attend to fractions and pounds, shillings and pence and the father would be responsible for long division, adding and subtraction and the decimal point. Weights and measures would be kept, along with the plotting of the graph and the nine times table, till a later time when he would concentrate on all the multiplication tables.

Henry, prowling round the bedroom, glanced at the dressing table as if some hidden monster had left his life and was breathing under the writing paper. Henry felt free (because of the letter from Mr H.) to write a careful invitation, and a careful little report on Muriel *and* her condition *and* a repeated suggestion that time was passing very quickly and arrangements had to be discussed.

He hoped, he wrote, that Mr H. could come quickly, after church, for Sunday dinner and perhaps stay for the rest of the day. They were all looking forward to having Mr H. for the day. Henry, as gently as possible, wanted to settle what he called the predicament as soon as possible. He wanted Mr H. to know that he, Henry, was not upper or lower class, he was, instead, an educated intellectual and outside the class system. He was not surprised at the turn of events. Mr H. was, indeed as he always thought, an innocent man. He was an honourable man and Henry wanted him to know that he, Henry, looked up to him. 'I mean,' he said to the tired face reflected in triplicate, 'Mr H. must be skilful to get Muriel pregnant without her knowing it.' This was said aloud for Muriel and her mother to hear in the kitchen. There was no response. He went on talking to his three faces.

Mr H., he said, must have known the basics, the birds and the bees stuff. Surely all Nannies had their little stories, *warning stories*, which Henry, not having a Nanny, had never had. But he knew well enough what not to do, till the right time. He supposed 'right times' were not provided in the lives of some people. He went on, he wanted Mr H. to know that he was grateful to Mr H. for cherishing Muriel. He explained that Muriel was innocent as well. She was unable, and this was not her fault, she was unable to understand the space between simple, gentle good manners and love. More than anything, Henry wanted Mr Hawthorne to come to Sunday dinner, the meal, Muriel's mother insisted, was luncheon and not a dinner. The more he thought about it the more he wanted Mr H. to be coming to Sunday dinner as usual. He wanted someone to look up to for advice. He wanted to speak, with permission, to an Officer and a Gentleman. He wanted someone (Mr H.) to speak to him; 'I've been a cad, sir,' and mean it. He wanted to shake hands with Mr Hawthorne. And, at the same time, the troubled intellectual, the giver of freedom, the questionable, whispered,

'Freedom' the whispered words, 'I was an Accessory', even before the Officer and Gentleman had finished his admission, his own confession would emerge.

While dipping his pen in the ink and writing with his best writing to invite Mr H., he could scarcely see the words on the page through his tears.

Henry envisaged the whole scene in advance. Mr H. would be serious and delicately truthful and even sorry, but halfway in the sense that, given the same chance, he might not restrain himself and refuse the invitation. And then there was Muriel wanting Mr Hawthorne, she desired him, Henry knew her well enough to know this.

'Do you understand?' Henry asked Mr H. in his note. It is not possible to have intense feelings of desire for two people at the same time.

Mr Hawthorne had impeccable good manners and a special code for living, with certain honourable rules.

Henry wrote that he was sure Mr Hawthorne's school motto would have been something like:

'Truth and Honour – Freedom and Courtesy.'

Many human errors and corrections fell within words

set out like that – add a little sentence, an explanation, 'that Freedom is not simply having your own way'. Even if Mr Hawthorne considered marriage, it must be remembered that Muriel was Henry's headache. She belonged to Henry.

Henry wanted, more than ever, to have Mr H. for Sunday dinner as he used to come. He realised Mr H. was in London and one simply did not travel all that way for Sunday dinner.

While dipping his pen and trying to write, he had to understand that he was crying and was not able to see what he had written. He had cried, silently, in the night, feeling insignificant and boring. He even thought of himself as an oaf in an elementary school, not as class captain but as the ink monitor. He tried to think of his class of boys and to prepare some drama for them to make a little performance, in class, in readiness for something bigger at the end of the year. He felt inadequate. He dipped his pen in the ink and let it dry. He pictured the scene of confrontation, possibly a time for celebration (he had worked out the possible dates for the expected birth of a son), someone to be taught differently from girls (daughters). Henry gave himself an artificial smile. How could he know if Mr Hawthorne would want him to teach his son? If this did come about, he would throw out the dressing table and have a desk with drawers and a leather top, worn with use (the desk would be second-hand). He began to weep without sound. He had never, in his whole life, wept properly *with noise*. A strange thought. He cried because he would have to know that he loved Muriel but was unable to stop her from wanting Mr Hawthorne. And he would have to confess this to the man himself in a sort of apology; something given with a light but honest little laugh.

Henry really wanted Mr H. to visit. He would hear the Officer, the Gentleman, the Barrister, the Church-going Tennis and Bridge Player saying that he knew he had been a cad. What does a man do, he might ask, when confronted by a need for chivalry, the act of chivalry, the ideal Knight's devotion to service . . . of women . . . Henry would explain that Muriel wanted Mr Hawthorne, in the first and second person. '*Do you understand she wanted you? Muriel, my wife, I love her but I can't stop her wanting you. It's not your fault.*'

Henry finished off his letter. He felt comforted by simply writing to the man. He looked forward to a visit from Mr Hawthorne. Having Mr Hawthorne to share Muriel's pregnant months, the childbirth and the subsequent bad nights and the burned or forgotten meals and the washing, don't forget the washing . . . put like this it might even work out quite well.

For all he knew, Henry thought, Mr H. might have been very lonely during the slow passing of time at the weekends. After the first invitation to Sunday dinner (luncheon for Muriel's mother), he did not miss a single Sunday dinner-time, arriving promptly and then taking his leave at three o'clock in the socially accepted way, only staying on for the day and early supper when pressed by Henry. Being pleasantly mixed with the little family seemed to be just what Mr H. wanted. If only, Henry thought, if only there was a way to get Mr H. safely back from London – now.

To be the much loved and admired Uncle or Friend of either the husband or the wife was, after all, a way of living (Henry's rather weak phrase) in Germany and

Austria and, perhaps, in Hungary as well. Desire felt towards one of a pair of married people could be deflected into playful teasing and an excess of demonstrative charm. Henry, observing this on his travels as a younger man, could feel the hollowness of it but, all the same, could see the strength of long-lasting friendship through the needs of desire and the necessary remedy in delightful company and behaviour. Henry told Muriel, right at the start, before London, that if Mr H. wanted to read Goethe's *Werther* on Sunday afternoons, he, Henry, would take the little girls for a long bicycle ride or a ride with a long slow hill to be walked up, leaning heavily on the bicycles and pushing them slowly towards home.

Desire, Henry knew, could not be paid off so easily. Desire, that deeply disturbing wish to satisfy a need for complete surrender and the reaching of an understanding of the unknown limits of sexuality, either in oneself, *within oneself* and/or another person.

Wishing for Mr Hawthorne, Muriel felt that she had been plodding through several Sundays and the weeks in between. Henry announced, in the kitchen, that he had the milk horse and did anyone care for a riding lesson? He greeted his mother-in-law with a French kiss, that is, he explained, a Romantic Greeting from the fingertips. He offered Muriel's mother a sherry, which was declined immediately. He called the little girls to come riding but the bedroom door was slammed shut.

Henry left the two women in the kitchen and went to the dressing table upstairs. He had cleared the space earlier. He heard Muriel's mother correcting his vowels and explaining, just one more time, the social difference between luncheon and dinner. As before, she despaired of being able to lift him out of the working class, he belonged there so solidly. She sighed.

'There's a war on, Grannie,' Henry had come down for a better pen. 'There's a war on,' he said, 'and there's bigger things to be thinking about.' He noticed Muriel's pale face. He almost asked her if she was 'unwell'. She would tell him, in time, he thought, as he went back up to the bedroom with a new pen and the inkwell.

'Oh, Mother, do be quiet,' he heard Muriel's complaining voice. 'There's nothing wrong with me.'

He poured himself a hidden glass of sherry. It was too cheap for his mother-in-law, and from the wrong country. He knew he must talk to Muriel, an intimate talk. He was not a fool.

He heard them in the kitchen. 'He's still drinking,' from Muriel's mother.

'He hasn't anything much to drink,' Muriel's voice.

'Oil or talcum, dearie?'

Henry, dressed only in a bath towel of doubtful freshness, sighed; 'You tell me.' He uttered the platitude to round off the transaction of clichéd shame which had started with the black-market sherry and a suggestion of gin (same source). A descent which had started without any intentions but which might, in an unwelcome way, continue. So far the arrangement had consumed not only the week's butter ration but threatened now to clear away any remaining money from the Savings Bank Jar concealed under the bed in the front bedroom. It was an opening to a life hitherto unknown.

'Full massage, is it? Or just a quick relief job to clear away the cobwebs?'

'Oh, you decide. You're the expert.' Henry, so much reduced, was grateful to his Jack, or should it be *Jill, of all trades?* In a previous cliché-ridden dialogue, Madame Tonks (retired) had soothed her client with one platitude after another (for example *not being able to see the wood for the trees*), and, for Henry, she understood perfectly that *no birds sang.*

'Relax, relax,' the scratchy gramophone voice told him with confidence, to 'relax and relax' while the claw-like hands searched his vulnerable one-woman-virginity and Mme Tonks, capable and sympathetic, smoothed more 'Ashes of Violets' over his shrinking flesh. He almost slept but the session was over. They were once again Mrs Tonkinson and Mr Bell. Henry, promising a home-grown, off-the-land cabbage, kissed his kindly neighbour and darted across the rough clinker of the unfinished road to his own home.

Henry read through his letter. He paused and then started to write, only to pause again. It was true, he had not heard the birds singing and his ability to write was really impaired. He understood this was because of present unhappiness. He was completely out of step with his own family life. He wished that Mr H. could visit often. He continued with his letter: 'I blame myself,' he wrote, 'if blame is needed. I'd rather see the whole thing falling into place without any real harm to anyone.' He went on to write that Mr H., his presence, was very much needed. He wanted to remind Mr H. that the weeks, following one after the other, were going by very fast. 'Ruthlessly,' he wrote, 'astonishing speed,' on towards 'full term', 'you understand the implication?' 'Arrangements have to be made, *must be made*.'

'How can you be so calm?' Muriel, leaving her mother downstairs, asked Henry. 'How can you write to Mr H.? How can you think that someone like him, with his standards, could or would make a young woman pregnant?' Muriel began to cry again. She cried for the cot and the pram and the baby clothes to come back. 'I should never have given them away, that's what's brought this on.' She cried some more for Mr Hawthorne.

Henry, interrupting, said he had no comments to make on middle-aged seduction. He said that Muriel should tell him who the father was. He took quick sips of sherry, despising himself and the drink, saying, 'Who is the father then?' in a voice not his own. 'A regular traveller on the London train? A city man with his black bowler hat, his briefcase and his man's umbrella, that light circular canopy of rich black silk rolled up to be carried as something special? A commercial traveller? More in your style?'

Henry, facing a truth, was frightened of his own unkindness. He was aware that the words were not his but, in reality, Mrs Tonkinson's explanation, *the alcohol speaking*. He was frightened of the power of alcohol, he knew this from boyhood. He had unwillingly witnessed the effects of what his father spoke of as the Devil's Bottle. He wanted now a little peace during which he could look over his letter to Mr H. – and then to write up the red notebook, especially with a reminder about not wasting money and some facts for discussion with Mr H. Muriel had agreed with the idea of two children only and was a passive member of any league against alcohol pursued by Henry. She understood that Henry was afraid, deeply afraid of not having enough money. Because of this she made herself little plans of economy. She had even joined in on the school camp. Being an organiser of a school camp brought in a little separate pay packet. That sort of thing pleased them both.

'The child should be able to visit his father often,' Henry was saying, looking up from his closely written pages. At the birth of a baby, Henry would often remind Muriel that the parents were looking at thirty-two years of responsibility. Neither of them had anything to say to this.

Pale and sweating, Henry had been going to be full of funny remarks and jokes for this conversation. He had been all set to pat Muriel's still flat stomach, calling her an experienced healthy multipara. Looking and feeling crushed, he simply said that when Mr H. replied to his letter they, himself and Muriel, must be prepared to offer the best way in which to proceed; the children must be brought up in the best ways needed for their well-being.

Henry knew, all along, that this freedom he had allowed in his marriage would not be looked upon in the same way by the very few people they knew as friends and, in particular, his own mother and father and, more pressingly, Muriel's mother and her own self-concerned attitude which needed no encouragement from anyone.

In spite of being shocked by his own behaviour, Henry was unable to give up or give way to an impossible situation. He stood up and pointed a finger at Muriel.

'I know,' he said. 'The father's a tramp in the air-raid shelter? A waiter in the hotel? The doorkeeper and the porter? Or even perhaps Florestan not able to recognise Leonore (in men's clothing) on his way out of the dungeon, on his way to the quartet – the music of recognition and of tenderness, the famous quartet. Come on, Muriel, be honest please. At least be honest. We always said we would be truthful to each other. Have you forgotten that music, the quartet, our love for each other which could never change?'

Muriel stared at Henry. His eyes were red and swollen. His voice was not quite his own. And, when he stood up, he swayed and had to sit down.

'A man can cry,' he said. 'And I'm crying now.' He sat on the edge of the bed and put both hands over his face. 'Tell me now,' he said. 'Tell me now who is the father. I have the correct dates. I want to know who is the father so that I can write the whole letter and invite him to come to Sunday dinner after church.'

Henry knew, all along, that this freedom in the marriage, so-called freedom in their marriage, really encouraged a decadence, a deterioration, a turning away alongside the standards of an artistic decadence which, before they were married, he and Muriel had both believed in and been refreshed by their belief.

Certain books, paintings, wall hangings, curtains and a second-hand carpet for the sitting room all had to be absolutely plain. No meaningless designs. They, in their youthful faithfulness, spending as little as possible, tried to achieve the silent, well thought of result in their limited space in their part of the divided house (a wartime block of flats made from an ordinary house).

Furniture too was 'utility' (wartime furniture), for those who were still, in their youth, unfurnished. Wartime furniture was neither beautiful nor offensively ugly. Books, practically being given away on the street barrows, brought another desired effect to the living arrangements. Henry and Muriel were slow to shelve their books. Mostly these strangers to the small house were piled in their correct, possessive shabbiness behind the sofa and the armchair where they could be seen and approved of, helpless as they were without shelves.

Muriel was greatly impressed by the aesthetic quality of clothes which were far removed from the good quality materials used in homemade blouses, dresses and skirts. Banished were the homemade lace curtains and the knitted tassels and bobbles and the heavy cable-stitch of home-knitted pullovers. Factory-new, smooth, woollen garments, and their cotton and linen counterparts, had a certain well-bred elegance enhanced by subdued colours and a new, short, fashionable hem length, a general shaping governed entirely by wartime economy.

Earlier, when they were first married, their enthusiasm for creating a happy and pretty house was their main reason for living, and the subject of all conversation. Henry paused at intervals to make notes in his special red notebook, the two main entries being the dates of the conceptions of the two baby girls and ultimately their birth dates and their first measurements in length and weight. At that time they lived in an old house which was divided into little flats or apartments; this gave them a sense of being progressive and modern with a wide knowledge and fondness for literature, including, especially, both ancient and present-day writers.

They handled music in this way as well, professing perhaps a little doubtful pleasure with modern classical music. They had in their share of the house one good-sized room, the living room, and a much smaller bedroom and the use of a shared kitchen and bathroom. They took turns to clean the bathroom and to tidy the kitchen. In this way they escaped from the conventional and the respectable. Banished were the floral cushions, the anti-macassars of homemade lace, the veiled flower-laden hats, the foxy furs and the table runners of fringed plush.

It was at this time that the tweed (Harris) jacket came into Henry's life, the leather elbows and the wrist bindings, as he said, as good as new. Taking themselves seriously, they had, early on in their marriage, discussed views on the merits of being married to one person for a whole lifetime. They were surprisingly close to each other in most considerations. One being that the number of children born should not exceed the amount of money put aside every week to be available for their children and their expenses in the future. Henry was adamant that there would be no more than two children.

Then there was the teaching of their own children and the great advantage, in Henry's opinion, as time went by, that the children, the two little girls as they grew older, could make friends and keep company, within limits, with Victor. This came second only to their music.

It was important, Henry often said, the children should be protected or shielded, but only to a certain extent. They must be acquainted with the sad and the difficult as well as the happy and the good. To be acquainted, not too much, with a cripple like Victor was good for them. To see Victor overcome his difficulties, as much as he could, was a tremendous lesson for the little girls. They must know something of the human condition. He then felt that this included the relationship with the grandmother. In Henry's private thought she was an example of a person who has to be tolerated, as kindly as possible, of course, and his daughters were already clever at knowing this in an unspoken way.

In the present circumstances Henry felt he should admit his own fault in the handling of freedom within a marriage. He felt he owed his confession to certain people in the Estate. He felt he should tell them about the new baby as if the whole thing was his mistake, his wrongdoing. He envisaged a series of doorstep confessions in which he would be perfectly honest. This would include Victor's place on the little footbridge. He had been surprised when Victor, after being away for quite some time, returned. Henry supposed he was 'between foster homes'. In his moments of uncertainty Henry tried, as he said to himself, to sort himself out and make decisions. His first decision was, there and then, to leave the official care of Victor to the good specialists who were trained and paid to 'keep eyes', as Muriel's mother would say, on Victor.

Muriel's unexpected and rather late pregnancy had been told seriously to the two little girls, from the landing at the top of the stairs. Henry, instead of reading the usual bedtime storybook outside their open doors, invented a sort of preliminary chapter covering the brave journey of Mr Sperm, who was the first of hundreds of competitors to reach Mrs Egg. He made the unforgivable error, he realised almost at once, of using real people and in particular the girls' own mother's name.

The children, in a sort of self-created false excitement, kept Henry there on the landing when he was far too tired, and long after the time when they, both girls, should have been asleep.

They rummaged in a wilderness of thoughts and childishly imagined scenes. They wanted to know did pigs all have baby pigs stored up inside them. And did rats have rats inside them?

'Tell us a mother-pig and a mother-rat story,' they said, and they wanted to know was Miss Tonks, once upon a time, folded up small inside Mrs Tonks. And with silly laughing, they danced on the beds, calling out, asking was their mother, once upon a time, inside their grandmother?

'Oh, Henry, for heaven's sake!' Muriel was angry. 'Can't you see the brats are leading you on. They'll take Ages to settle down. Such a silly subject to push on them just now.'

She was coming upstairs, she called out to the children. She called to them it was time to be quiet and to go to sleep.

'Yes, pigs do have baby pigs inside them,' she said. 'A mother pig might have six little baby pigs inside her.' She told the little girls to think about the sweet little baby pigs waiting to be born. 'Pretend you are baby pigs and go to sleep.'

Muriel was on the way up the narrow stairs as Henry was coming down. She put an arm round Henry, to steady herself, she explained. She had to tell him, she said, that she found it impossible to believe he could be so foolish in exciting the wakeful little girls. She wanted. She needed to get to bed, in a bed by herself. Did he get that? she wanted to know. He was to put the little girls in the bed together when they were asleep. Edging away from him, she told him she must have a room and a bed to herself. *Did he get that? she wanted to know.* And now he must listen, she said, when they were both in the small front hall. He must be mad, she told him, to want to go round the Estate telling perfect strangers (if there were actually any other people in the other houses) about the baby. 'I don't want to be talked about all over the Estate.' Muriel told Henry she just could not understand him.

223

He must manage his guilt or his jealousy or whatever it was, some other way.

'Mother's leaving,' Muriel said, 'I told her you would go with her to the bus.'

'I go alone to bus,' Muriel's mother's voice intruded. 'Let him cringing on doorstep if he want. I go alone to bus.'

'What will people think of us?' Muriel said in a tearful voice. Henry said that people seeing him taking her mother to the bus would think 'What a nice young man that is! They would all queue up to go to the bus.'

'Remember and remember,' Muriel said, 'I like and really need sensitive good manners.'

'Muriel, what do you mean?' Henry, shocked by the hatred in her voice, sounded as if he was near tears.

'You'll know soon enough,' Muriel said. 'Good manners would get me off this staircase. And good thoughtful manners would see that there was a room for me and an empty bed for me to sleep in *alone*.'

Henry, skilled in moving sleeping children, put both little girls into one bed. 'I'm off to the bus with your mother,' he called out. 'Empty bed awaits you!'

'Let him cringe on doorstep,' Muriel's mother's voice penetrated the night. 'I go alone to bus.' Henry, feeling a distaste created by himself, was trapped. He saw the ugly line of Muriel's mother's mouth, unfriendly, in the weak light of his pocket torch. He thought of his small innocent house able to deal with any problem which might be waiting to show itself. This was the way to think of his house . . .

It was a very dark night, of course no lights from windows and no street lamps. The misery, Henry confessed to himself, was all selfish, wretched and stupid in the face of the progress and suffering of the war. He was powerless in this dark street. But, he told himself, he was not powerless in his own house, his own *rented* house. He must not put himself too high on the list of the powerful. He was the family man. He was hungry but not for food. He wanted revenge of some sort. He would let Muriel sleep alone, he had allowed her two nights away with Mr H. while he had remained at home alone in the house with two self-willed, adventure-mad little girls. He needed a rest and a change and Muriel needed a reminder about her husband's thoughtfulness and generosity. Her well-being was never forgotten. He knew from childhood experience that women needed beating or frequent authoritative treatment. Though the thought disgusted him, he would go straight home and then, as if in fun, he would punish her. Not a slap in the face, that would be too much of a shock. He would, he thought, give her a light punch on the nose. That was it, not to break her nose but simply to hurt her a bit and to cause her nose to bleed. He told himself to go straight up to the bedroom, her nose could bleed on to her raggy nightdress, that would be better than spoiling her dress. He smiled at the thought.

He was out of breath, his legs felt weak. He was running all the way down the street. His mind made up.

Henry, in the kitchen, was surprised by the trembling weakness in his hands and legs. He could hardly breathe enough. He groaned aloud as though an illness had him in a dreadful final embrace. It was the idea of revenge which made him, he thought, feel ill. He was not capable of revenge. He was hungry. Of course that was it. In his fit of hunger he ate the whole week's cheese ration. And he ruined the loaf by chewing it at both ends instead of finding the bread knife and cutting neat slices. He sat a few minutes, the quick meal was just what he needed. He was ready now to go upstairs to Muriel to show her who was the senior officer in the establishment. Who gives and who receives the salute? It would be all for her own good, as his dad always said. Henry felt that he was an echo through the years, holding the same useful sentiments. He was also like an animal in that the food had made him want to sleep. He remembered that there was no bed for him. He would have to sleep on the couch and be all bent and stiff in the morning. He thought about Mr Hawthorne. He remembered a moment of meeting, nameless in the small quiet hours after an all-night air-raid warning. They had both been on duty in the same area. They stopped, with relief, in the street to exchange greetings. Remembering the quick detail, Henry, at the time, thought how peaceful and noble this other man was, with his refined good manners and charm, the whole scene enhanced in the tender light of the sunrise. He thought now that Mr H. would most likely have looked like this on the morning of conception. He had, himself, the experience, the responsibility of the 'transfiguration of Muriel'. He still *Blessed himself* for making her radiant and lovely.

Sounds of fingers tapping and scrambling on the window disturbed Henry's sleep. The fire was almost out. This was no time for visitors. All the same he opened the door. The shawled figure was not hard to identify. Henry started to explain that he was sleeping on the sofa and that ladies' hairdressing and dressmaking were hardly required at this time of night, 'not even a quick massage, thank you very much.'

Mrs Tonkinson did not waste time, she had brought him a present, no it couldn't be seen, it was in her head and she had taken the trouble because his lights were showing all the way down to Dover as usual.

'I brought pins and a bit of spare blackout stuff. I'll fix up the curtings a bit better for you. You don't want to be fined just now, do you? A course not!'

Henry was touched and pleased. He knew he really needed visitors, someone thoroughly talkative and out-spoken. He felt comforted. As for teaching Muriel a lesson, he had crept away from her bed without waking her, let alone a punishment . . . 'I'm pleased to see you, Mrs T.,' Henry said.

'It isn't all I came over for,' Mrs Tonks settled herself in the armchair. 'Make up the fire, there's a good lad, and yes I could do with a cup of tea. Put the kettle on, I brought me own teapot, there's some tea just here, just needs a hotting up.' The well-used teapot rattled on the table. The visitor nodded with approval as the fire, under the black coal dust, came to life. She plunged straight into the reason for her nocturnal visit. She told Henry he must let Muriel work through the experience, 'but let her take her own time, with us all helping her, bit by piece.'

She drank her tea. 'She'll be orlright and the Gentleman as you know him, he is a real Gentleman – and will do all the right things by you and her and you must not be too proud to take what he'll give. You must take a holt of it. You must all find ways to fit together, different ways with lovin' harmony like a nice romance, a film or a story.' As if reading Henry's mind, Mrs Tonkinson leaned forward and told him that she didn't hold with divorce. She explained that the woman divorces the man, even if the woman is in the wrong. 'The man comes out of it the worse, money wise and every way.' A case is made against the man. 'Because, my darlin', men is regarded as the guilty party no matter who's done what to ruin the marridge mental cruelty gets cooked up into a nice little dish. Many men is soft and innocent and would not hurt a fly and they're expected to see themselves as "mentally cruel". You can't teach in school if divorced . . . '

Mrs Tonkinson, masseuse, fortune-teller, hairdresser (Ladies) and dressmaker knew when to make dramatic pauses. Henry, kneeling to coax the fire, had to wipe the tears off his face with coal dust all over his hands. Mrs

Tonks could not help a shrill cackle of a laugh, 'Pardon me for laughing,' she said and they both listened. No sound came from upstairs. 'Yo'll have to wash your face,' she told him. 'Take your time,' she said.

'I'm in no hurry,' she said, pouring a little gin into her teapot.

'Get washed in the sink there,' the visitor said, 'and I'll come to the real reason for my visit. I'll take a drop more out of your kettle to mend my pot.'

Henry hardly knew what to say. He felt that all their plans, both his and Muriel's, their youthful plans, for the right books and pictures, the plain carpet, especially the elegance of the plain carpet, were about to count for nothing like some childish whim . . .

'There's many ladies, let me remind you,' Mrs Tonks said, 'ladies well established in their places in society, there's many a lady left with a little white towelling bundle and a neat little black bank book. Need I say more? White fluffy bundles and neat little black books. Remember, some money, at certain times, does grow on trees.'

Henry wanted to say that their, himself and Muriel's,

situation was entirely different. For one thing Mr H., H short for Hawthorne, was a much-loved family friend, and this friendship would continue without standing up for opinions. Tonks, you must understand that. Mrs Tonks nodded, she agreed. And then set off on her reason for coming, the point about Mr H. being of importance. She then went on to explain to Henry about Mr Hawthorne and the family life which included him. As she, Mrs Tonks, saw the picture, that part presented very little difficulty if Henry could see his own part clearly and live by that. The hardest part was Henry's because of the power of jealousy. This power could ruin them all if Henry was not able to be larger than his jealousy – this jealousy being a natural part of a person's personality. Some more than others. 'That's how I see it.' Mrs Tonkinson sat back from the somewhat close and earnest position she had adopted. 'The present I've brought you can't be wrapped up with coloured paper. It's in my head,' Mrs Tonks said. 'I have to come with it that's why I'm here. It's especially for the creation of understanding and feeling, the emotional – it's a speech but is more like a pome. '*Is whispering nothing?*' she began.

> '*Is leaning cheek to cheek? is meeting noses?*
> *Kissing with inside lip? Stopping the career of*
> *Laughter with a sigh? – a note infallible*
> *Of breaking honesty; horsing foot on foot?*
> *Skulking in corners? Wishing clocks more swift?*
> *Hours, minutes? noon, midnight? and all eyes*
> *Blind with pin and web but theirs only,*
> *That would unseen be wicked? Is this nothing?*
> *The covering sky is nothing; Bohemia nothing?*
> *My wife is nothing; nor nothing have these nothings,*
> *If this be nothing.*

Mrs Tonkinson sat down. Henry said the recitation was excellent, so honest and full of meaning. The hopelessness of jealousy, and the pain of jealousy, the overpowering strength of jealousy as if written by the real owner of jealousy; and the way in which an ugly aspect of the personality can be transformed into an honest and known emotion and, in this way, is controlled. He took her in his arms and kissed her.

Later in the day Henry crossed the rough road to take a cabbage to Mrs Tonkinson.

'Give us a kiss then? Oo's got a kiss for me? I'd like to read that Shakespeare play again,' Mrs T. told Henry, who promised to bring the book, knowing that she was capable of propping up the kitchen-table leg with it, not just as a temporary measure, but forever.

$\mathcal{M}$uriel was resting. She had fourteen days 'lying in' after the birth, in the Town Cottage Hospital. (Henry faithfully added all the details in the red notebook.) And then, as a present from her mother, she had two weeks in a nursing home. Mr H. sent flowers and chocolate rations to both places but had, discreetly, not visited. He arrived, as expected, this day at Henry's invitation, to afternoon tea and for supper. Because Muriel cried so much, saying she had nothing to wear, her smocks being worn out and washed to death, her mother went shopping by herself and bought a costume, a jacket and skirt, for her. It was something they had seen together, but Muriel had never thought she might possess. Muriel had not even tried it on because of her size being altered by her condition. The costume was of a very good quality fine woollen cloth, a pale misty-green for the skirt and the same for the jacket, which had, as well, some little cherry-coloured squares woven into the cloth. A soft little white blouse would go just right with the costume, Leonie said. Leonie on a friendly but unexpected visit looked at the costume with reverence. On a recent unexpected visit, Leonie, with her usual candour, had described Henry (fortunately he was out) as being, in her opinion, sexually chaste; and that for all his fierce looks he was as amiable as a seaside donkey. And, she said she could see, she always said, how suitable he was for Muriel. 'Low-key sex,' she said then, just enough to get a baby. Nothing more. On this same occasion, Leonie thought it useful to explain to Muriel that most men, especially Henry, do not like criticism of any sort. A man, in thoughts about himself, is never wrong. Men, Leonie said, find it hard to say something to show an apology.

As Muriel's mother often said, one should never do or say anything which needs an apology. Because Mr H. was expected, Muriel did not try to invite Leonie. Leonie, Muriel was wise to understand, invited herself. She was often useful for conversations of an intimate sort and usually visited just when the idea prompted her. She saw herself, Henry at one time tried to explain to Muriel, Leonie saw herself as a natural necessity and Muriel should be careful with such a person. 'Especially,' Henry said, with his arm steadying Muriel, who was frail from so much postnatal resting on beds, 'don't bring out the costume if she is here.'

'Whyever?' Muriel was surprised, but something in Henry's voice was warning her.

It was a sort of ritual fight, an establishment of seniority with certain rules made up and understood. They had been having afternoon tea in the most well-mannered way, using Muriel's mother's real china, when all at once Mr Hawthorne addressed Henry and asked him to step outside into the garden. The little girls, after playing their violins for the guests, were granted permission to take the new baby, a boy who looked like Mr H., for a little walk in his new pram.

'May the best man win.' A voice was heard to start the proceedings. Mr Hawthorne got Henry at once into a headlock and was about to release him when it was clear that the women had come into the garden (a few flower petals demonstrated 'garden' together with the cabbages, remaining, but past their best).

'Not before the Ladies!' Mr Hawthorne's low voice was just heard, and then louder, 'The Ladies are joining us.'

Henry, unexpectedly caught, he realised, having been to the wrong kind of school, wriggled free from the older and heavier man and ran 'trip trip' backwards from his opponent on 'tippy toes', 'as if in a ballet,' Muriel called out in laughter. Henry, his face rather an unpleasant purple, judged himself to be far back enough and so, with muscle and trained breathing, he ran at his adversary, his antagonist, and head-butted him, causing a surprised and pained gasp followed by a folding forward movement of the said well-built gentleman.

Dotty Tonks, with a homemade megaphone, declared the fight to be a tie and may the best men remain as they are.

Both little girls wanted to push the pram but had to take turns.

'Take the pram in turns,' Muriel called out from the cake she was cutting. 'Anyone fighting, no one takes him.'

'Not even Daddy?'

'Don't be silly. Who would quarrel with Daddy over the pram?'

'You and Daddy of course. You're always in an argu-ment! And Daddy and Mr H. often want the same thing, they . . . '

'That's enough, go for your walk and be careful. And take turns about, be good girls!'

Muriel sighed. Too many people seemed to be attached to this baby. She longed to sit nursing him her-self. He was called The Baby, or Baby or The Boy, Himself or The Babby (Mrs Tonkinson), My Prince (Tonkette – herself a Princess and film star). 'Beauty is sometimes,' Muriel's mother joined in, 'Beauty is some-times ravaged by too much make-up. Plastered! I would like to say go wash yourself . . . But no one listens.'

'If anyone should call to visit us,' the elder daughter announced at breakfast time, 'Please tell them,' she said to her father, 'that we are at school. We shall be school every day. All day and every day.'

Henry said he would pass on the message. Already disappointed with a failed poem, he felt a deep sadness because being at school seemed to be the desired thing, when studying at home was, to him, the best blessing a child could have. Especially, he thought, the fresh experiences, every day, would be so stimulating and they would be working steadily ahead instead of being held back by the class and the irritation of slow progress and subsequent boredom.

It seemed to Henry that the girls had dressed themselves in some garments resembling the school uniform, the schoolgirl's tunic which was worn over a nice clean blouse. Reminded of his own schoolyard childhood, he smiled at the daughters' choice of clothing. He then remembered that Mrs Tonks, when clearing her house, had passed on two gym tunics, 'as there was plenty of wear in them for the little girls to grow into'. They were clearly too large, the tunics, and the girdles, the woven braid-like belts, had been tied tightly low down and the tunics pulled up into sort of crude bags of cloth, a looping of surplus material only just held up and off the ground in a most awkward way.

Of course no one came to visit and the girls did not go to school. To divert them Henry told them to go to the cot and sing to the baby.

'See if you can make him happy. And, take off those big dresses. Sooner or later,' he said, 'you'll trip over them.'

Left alone, Henry tried to concentrate on his poem. Muriel, after a disturbed night, was tired; she tried not to be disagreeable. She said that she knew the little girls had grown quite a lot but the tunics were far too big for them and she, Muriel Bell, was not going to unpick seams and hems and do the necessary sewing to make the ugly tunics wearable. Especially as the girls would probably not want to wear them . . .

Could they put little little Leopold into the dolly pram the little girls wanted to know. 'Can we? Can we?'

Muriel, because she loved this baby so much, felt she must make up to the little girls. She loved the baby. She was happy with him. She picked him up and, knowing it was not the best thing, she put him gently in the doll's pram.

'Just in the hall, that's all. Just wheel him up and down in the hall,' she said.

Muriel had been pleased and impressed when the little girls had, in turn, actually learned how to pick up the baby – his head supported and in line with the rest of his manly little body. His perfect little body. She went to have a rest.

The baby, named at once 'Leopold' by Henry, was so perfect. In her thoughts she fitted him to the man whose child he was. She could not endure his unhappiness but would gather him to her breast whenever he cried, seeing his distress in the movement of his tiny arms and legs.

'He must cry,' the Visiting Nurse told Muriel. 'When he kicks and cries, he is body building,' she said, 'and remember he is trying to learn and to establish where you, his mother, are.'

The house was quiet, Muriel turned softly on her bed

and wished for a few more minutes' sleep. She was sinking into the softness.

Perhaps it was the quietness of the house which roused her. She rolled over and off the bed.

Meanwhile the dolly pram was racketing along the path by the stormwater drain.

'Take the little pram back to the house and wheel the big pram,' Henry told the children. 'The baby should not be rattled and shaken like that.'

Both the little girls wanted to push the pram, a real pram not a dolly pram. This pram rolled *smooth smooth* alongside the water all the way to the little footbridge. They were to wait there for their father.

The new baby slept with his arms up, one fist on either side of his almost bald little head. The little girls told each other how much they loved the baby brother. They took off their shoes and socks and cooled their feet in the stream. Their father, when he came, said that they could hang upside down on the bridge while he walked in the fields.

Leopoldi (Henry's name for the baby) might like to

have his feet in the cool water, the sisters agreed. Together they undressed him carefully, remembering that his little head needed supporting on the delicate stalk of the tiny neck.

Henry, walking on the fresh-scented grass, tried to overcome feelings of anger and depression; mostly he was sad and worried. He knew he liked order and all, at present, was out of order. He wished for the company of Mr H. That friendship had many good things, but he stood still, seeing nothing. There was far too much for the red notebook. Life, it seemed, was bowling them over. 'Pardon,' he said to the grassy field. 'There won't be enough money . . .'

'Can Leopoldi paddle? Daddy?' the younger daughter was tugging his arm. 'Please, Daddy, come.' Henry grabbed her arm. Her face was flushed and tears were coming fast. He heard the baby's shrill crying. He ran, and in order to be quick he left the little girl standing in the field.

'I've been such a silly fool,' Henry ran and ran, it seemed a long way, a nightmare especially as there were no more sounds of the baby crying. Drowning, the silent death, he told himself, he would welcome life without complaining – or without even expecting anything for himself, if only this baby boy, this beautiful child was safe there by the bridge. He understood completely that the little girls would have wanted to give the baby brother a special treat. They would have decided to dip his little pink feet in the cold water. Still running, Henry, in his thoughts, begged some kind of god to save the precious child. He felt he was too slow and unable to make the short distance in time. He thought he could see someone on the bridge. The baby was no longer crying.

'Too late,' he needed to stop and breathe. He saw the elder sister holding the baby while someone, not Muriel, was effectively putting a shawl round the little creature. He could not think who was there.

It was Victor. He must have been under the bridge all the time. Henry could not thank him enough. Victor, with a flourish, waved. Gentle, quick Victor.

Leopoldi, flat in the pram, made his little creaking sounds of pleasure. He seemed completely soothed by the

movement of the pram. They were interrupted. Mr Hawthorne and Muriel had come as Mr H. had to leave for his
train. Henry said he would go with him to the station,
the girls could take their mother and the baby home.

Mr Hawthorne, as expected, had quietly been very
generous with expenses for the baby son. He had been
very quiet and thoughtful and had not complained about
a lonely existence which waited for him. Henry imagined
how lonely Mr H. could be and told him to come in to
the family whenever he had time and inclination.

Leopoldi spent his days in the pram showing early
signs of intelligence and continued comfort. Henry was
pleased to note these qualities in his notebook. Especially
noteworthy was, because of the strength of this baby,
Muriel found she was able to breastfeed him. Henry,
looking on, did not reveal any jealousy though he felt it
acutely at times.

Tea, real tea freshly made, Mr Hawthorne having
brought, as a precious gift in silver wrapping paper, a

packet of tea. Miss Dotty Tonks, the Tonkette, revealed that she had been able to make a fruit cake with dried fruit hoarded for a whole year.

The two men, the Cad and the Accessory, faced each other. They clasped each other by the hand. They shook hands, with some roughness of embarrassment in their throats, and agreed that in spite of a weight difference, an educational difference, a noteworthy clan difference, a completely different set of mother and father each, they were accessible for a firm handshake, even for an attempt at the salute. Though Mr H. declared it was not necessary between family.

The costume was tried on, in the presence of Leonie, the next day. Leonie kept saying she had to help her friend, Muriel, her very Best Friend, there was no escape.

Leonie walked round and round saying she could not see exactly what was wrong with the clothes. The neckline, the shoulders and the waist of the jacket were all perfect, a perfect fit and a lovely blend of colours. Muriel, wishing for fresh clothes after wearing the same clothes,

the same cotton smocks day in and day out till Kingdom come,
was helpless in tears. She had not seen any pouching in
the lovely material. She showed them, in turn, Muriel's
mother and Henry and Mr Hawthorne, who had been
invited to come to dinner (luncheon, Muriel's mother
translated for Mr Hawthorne), before he had to return,
yet again, later to London.

Leonie asked for 'a loan' (her words) of some nail-
scissors or embroidery scissors. And quickly she snipped
at the green, silken thread; *snip clip snip clip* of the small
scissors and the lining, in freedom, slipped out below the
waistline of the jacket all silky and wrong. The whole suit
ruined while the family looked on in dismay.

'Nothing to worry about,' Leonie bundled up the
whole costume, saying that she would fix it. If it took a
bit more time Muriel would have to wait a bit. And the
next minute the visitor had gone. She, Muriel, seeing the
concern reflected in the eyes of both Henry and Mr
Hawthorne wanted, more than anything, to smile
bravely but her tears took over.

'Muriel needs to lie down for an hour,' Henry said to

Mr Hawthorne. 'Please take her upstairs and make her comfortable.'

Somehow the days went by with everyone in the new baby's world. Even Mr Hawthorne who had started missing his train, and even missing the late train, in order, it seemed, for him to take some time off with his little son.

In the new baby's world he dominated the mealtimes and shamelessly used up all the hot water at his bathtimes. Everyone liked being at his bath to watch him enjoying the warm water. It seemed as if this tiny slip of a child already liked to be admired. The little girls seemed to understand this and, in a gentle way, they splashed him with the bath water. They even understood that his mealtimes were tremendously important; they could tell, they explained, the different things he wanted from the different sounds he was able to make. The little girls were quick to know when mother and baby were best left alone together.

Muriel was pleased with the behaviour of the little

girls and told them she was pleased. The household, Henry said, was Blessed with the presence of Mr Haw- thorne's son. Henry explained that he had had no previous idea how a small new baby could have such an influence.

Muriel, it seemed to Henry, approved of the sweet idea of the house being blessed in this way. A continua- tion of 'her way of being' as she was before her life had become so much a duty rather than daily happiness. Henry, noticing the change in her, scribbled quickly in the notebook to keep the pleasure of it close by. He hoped they might come together once more in perfect understanding, but he held back out of a kind of rever- ence he had not expected. It was, he felt, as if her body was actually the property of someone else. He supposed it was, leaving Muriel aside, the father and son. He made notes and felt ashamed of his attitude towards Mr H., wishing for a return of affection from him. He supposed Muriel was, with her baby, able to put aside the adult affection. Muriel might even be wishing, he thought in silence, to have his arm across her while they slept. She might be needing, as he was, something intimate and close between them extra to the birth of Leopoldi.

He, Henry, thought and wrote, without saying anything because he thought that Muriel might be, without saying anything, she might be wanting him to stroke and caress her carefully in all the right places (which he knew so well), without saying anything, but careful, while her body was changing itself back to being without its recent special passenger. He knew Muriel and her body and her mind so well. Who could have more knowledge than he had?

Certainly not Mr H., but he was afraid of his thoughts. He was so, so afraid of his thoughts. He could never know what Mr H., with all his perfection, would or could be like as the Lover with all the secret ways of loving. And Muriel might be unable to stop wishing, all the time, for this other man's intimate and hidden language of love. They, himself and Muriel, had often spoken together in the dark about such things as if one or the other should have to be alone. It seemed to Henry that it would be possible to be prepared for being without any physical

feeling enhanced by the sweet deeply emotional movements offered by the arms and the hands and the body;
the rhythm of the body in love, culminating in pressing
the lips to the sweet thought of the wish of the moment.
But the loneliness . . .

But he was not alone. He was in bed with Muriel.
The house was quite quiet. He was alone and awake and
the baby was not crying.

Henry liked to think that German was being learned
by a few people. This was, at the present time, in the
progress of the war. Germans might feel honoured by
German classes in England . . .

On fine days people paused by the pram. The little girls
enjoyed showing off their baby.

Mrs Tonkinson, pausing and leaning over the pram,
turned to Henry as if with 'second sight', telling him that
the next baby would be a boy and would be his.

Muriel came to take the pram. She placed the baby
in the pram by the back door, and then she undressed

him to change his nappy and to admire him and his tiny penis. Mrs Tonkinson was telling Muriel not to weep near or over the baby.

'He'll grieve,' she told Henry and Muriel.

'He'll grieve,' she told them. 'He'll grieve while you grieve and he won't thrive.'

Muriel thought of the reliable little penis in the open air and all the responsibility attached in readiness . . . She almost cried and then remembered the warning.

Quotation from a letter written by Dostoevski on 27 March 1878, shortly before his death. (To a mother.)

Be kind and let your child understand that you are kind (by himself without any prompting) and let him always remember that you have been kind to him. Then, believe me, you will have fulfilled your duty towards him all through his life, because, without wishing to influence him in any way you have taught him that kindness is good. In that case he will remember you all his life with respect and even, perhaps, with a feeling of tenderness. And if you were ever guilty of any bad action, or at any rate thoughtless, painful or even ridiculous action, he will without a doubt, sooner or later forgive all your bad actions for the sake of the good ones, which he will remember. You cannot do anything more for him. Besides, this is more than enough. For the memory of anything good, – that is, the memory of kindness, truth, honesty, compassion, the absence of a false feeling of shame – as far as possible – of lies – all this will make a different man of him, sooner or later, be sure of that —

SOURCES

The author wishes to acknowledge the use of the following:

'The mind of man is framed even like the breath . . .' from Wordsworth the Poet. Poem: 'The Prelude', p. 10 from *Book One, Childhood and Schooltime*, lines 351–355. Published text of 1805, Introduction and Notes edited from manuscripts by Ernest de Selincourt. Editor Geoffrey Cumberlege, Oxford University Press, London, 1933.

Thomas Mann, *Buddenbrooks*, pp. 332–3. The translation was first published by Penguin Books, 1924; *Death in Venice* from *Stories and Episodes*, J.M. Dent & Sons Ltd, London, 1911.

Sir Samuel Johnson and Sir Walter Scott. Quote taken from 18 September 1768. Johnson's fear that 'to write a history' of his melancholy (which he never did) 'would too much disturb him' is again reminiscent of Scott. Compare Scott's Journal for 23 May 1830 (after he had discontinued it for almost a

257

year): 'I thought it made me abominably selfish, and that by recording my gloomy fits I encouraged their recurrence.'

Samuel Johnson, *Selected Writings*, edited by Patrick Cruttwell, Penguin English Library, Harmondsworth, 1968.

Quote: 'Is whispering nothing?' she began . . . (Mrs Tonkinson's present which cannot be wrapped up in gift paper but delivered by recitation.) *The Winter's Tale*, Act I, scene ii, by William Shakespeare, Swan Shakespeare comedies, J.M. Dent & Sons Ltd, London, 1930.

The quotation at the end of this book from a letter Dostoevski wrote to a young mother: I do not have the book any more. Several books, old ones, were burned with toys and furniture in the Great Fire we had in 1997. Years ago I had copied the passage, at some time, into my diary but failed to include the essential things!

Elizabeth Jolley, 2001